Mississippi History

STORIES BY

Steve Yarbrough

University of Missouri Press
Columbia and London

University of Missouri Press, Columbia, Missouri 65201
Printed and bound in the United States of America
5   4   3   2   1   98   97   96   95   94

Library of Congress Cataloging-in-Publication Data

Yarbrough, Steve, 1956-
    Mississippi history: stories/by Steve Yarbrough.
        p.   cm.
    Contents: House of health–Stay-gone days–Mississippi history–
Hungarian stew–Black angus–A life of ease–Hoe hands–The tower –
Hazel Baker.
    ISBN 0-8262-0967-X (paper)
    I. Title.
PS3575.A717M57   1994
813'.54–dc20   94-20134
                                                            CIP

∞™ This paper meets the requirements of the American National Standard
for Permanence of Paper for Printed Library Materials, Z39.48, 1984.

Designer: Rhonda Miller
Typesetter: Connell-Zeko Type & Graphics
Printer and Binder: Thomson-Shore, Inc.
Typefaces: Pepita and Palatino

For credits see page 157.

For Magda and Tosha, my darling daughters
Special thanks to T. R. Hummer and Michael Pinkston

Contents

*M*ississippi
History

*H*ouse of Health

Cooper's office is across the street from Indianola Hardware, in a building that used to be an appliance store. He has his waiting area out front, and all the treatment rooms and the x-ray equipment are in the back. Paperback racks are attached to the walls. They contain such books and pamphlets as *The Health Hazards of Ice Cream, Are You a Saltaholic?* and *The Biblical Foundations of Chiropractic.* A note taped to the front of each rack reads, "Please take as many as you need."

This morning, there's the regular array of suffering flesh inside. Two or three old ladies whose names I don't know and a guy named Slaughter, who got broadsided a few weeks ago at the intersection of 49 and 82. There's also a tall, red-headed woman named Sara Mitchell.

Slaughter and the old ladies ignore me when I walk in. Just as I feel my face start to flush, Sara says, "Good morning, James. How's Carol?"

Carol's my daughter. She's seventeen, a senior in high school. She's blonde and bright and almost eight months pregnant. Her boyfriend's gone to live in Montana with his uncle. Carol doesn't know exactly where he is, and if she did, she wouldn't tell me, because she'd be afraid I might drive up there and kill him. Most days I don't think I would, but some days I think I might. His father's dead, so I can't kill him. His mother knows I'd never hurt a woman, but she still heads the other way if she sees me on the street.

At the mention of Carol, Slaughter and the old ladies lean forward.

"She's doing pretty well," I tell Sara, sitting down beside her. "It's a hectic time, though. The baby's due, she's got

1

graduation coming up, I'm trying to break land."

"And it's been raining like the pipes up in the sky have sprung a leak," Sara finishes up. "You ought to put your land in fishponds, James. You're not quite so much at the mercy of the elements then."

Sara's the only woman catfish farmer I know of. She lives about halfway between Indianola and Leland. She's got three or four other women working for her, all of them living out there on her land. Sometimes you'll see two or three of them together at the Beer Smith Lounge, drinking Bud and shooting pool or playing shuffleboard. They're all about forty. They wear khaki work clothes and keep their hair cut short, but they're still nice-looking women.

You can probably imagine what most folks say about them, though. Southern Prime, the big catfish plant on the outskirts of town, wouldn't let Sara buy stock when she tried. She sells her fish to a black man who owns a processing plant up near Drew.

"I'd love to outsmart the elements," I tell her. "I just can't afford the start-up costs."

"Oh, it's a pain in the neck getting started," she says. "I'd be the last person in the world to deny that."

We sit together for almost half an hour, talking idly about the price of fish and the cost of preemergents, about the weather forecast and the new man who's taken over at Planters' Bank. A couple of folks leave, a couple more enter. One or two of them nod at us, but the others pretend neither one of us is here. We might as well be two empty chairs.

Cooper's wife finally steps into the waiting room and tells Sara she can come on back.

"See you later, James," Sara says. "You ever want to come out and look at my little operation, I'd be happy to show it to you. We've been able to keep our costs down. There's ways."

"Thanks," I say. "I might take you up on it."

A few minutes later it's my turn. I walk through the door and down the hall, past cardboard cartons of the herbs, charcoal, seawater, and other unusual remedies that Cooper prescribes for everything from warts to melanoma. Cooper's wife puts me in the third room on the right. Next door, Cooper's just finished adjusting Sara. "You get some rest now," he says.

Cooper's in his mid-forties, just like me. He's a thin, blond man who wears some of the worst clothes you ever saw. His pants are polyester double knits, always plaid, the kind I remember wearing to church back in the seventies, which is probably when he bought his. Cooper's not exactly fashion conscious.

I started coming to him right after my wife, Jackie, got killed in a car wreck. Carol was just five at the time, and she was waking up a lot at night, having bad dreams. I'd jump out of bed, run into her room and pick her up, and a couple of times when I did that, my back went out on me. One night the pain hit me so hard I ended up on the floor. The next thing I knew, Carol was screaming *"Daddy!"* and bending over me, her little hands clamped to her ears. The white light behind my eyes had almost struck me blind, but I could see her face clearly enough to realize she thought her dad was dead too.

I rarely feel that kind of pain anymore, but every now and then I get headaches, and my neck stiffens up. Within a few days the pain has spread to my lower back and legs, and if I don't make a visit to Cooper, I start having trouble just standing up and walking.

This morning Cooper has me sit on the adjustment table while he stands behind me and runs a calorimeter up my neck.

"Eight," he says.

He walks over to the desk where my chart lies and writes the number down. "That's the highest you've been in over two years."

"I'm feeling pretty tense, I guess."

"You need to relax more," Cooper says. "Why don't you come out this weekend and spend some time in my sauna? I've invited a couple of the other patients."

"Thanks," I say. "If it ever quits raining, I may have to spend the weekend in the field. Otherwise, I'll give you a call and come ahead."

He measures my leg-length—the right one's five-sixteenths shorter than the left today—then tells me to lie on my right side.

Standing inches away from my face, he lays his right hand gently on the side of my neck. He feels around till he finds the first vertebra. It's the one all the nerve channels pass through. He says that if you line it up right, everything else will fall into line too. He's right, I believe, but the problem is that you line it up and it stays in place for a little while and then it starts slipping again.

Cooper doesn't snap your bones—he's from a different school. He exerts pressure, fifty or sixty pounds of it, on his right forearm with his left hand, and the force is transferred to my neck through his fingers. His legs tremble while he presses on his arm, I can hear his joints cracking. But I never feel him making the adjustment.

When he's finished, he smiles and says, "Get a lot of rest, James. Sleep's the nicest gift you can give yourself."

Since I've pushed my credit line to the limit, sleep's about all I can afford to give myself, I think. Then it occurs to me that I can't really afford to give myself that either, at least not if it stops raining.

Outside, it's pounding down so hard I can barely see the street. I get soaked just walking to the pickup. I'm about to crank it when Sara Mitchell pulls up beside me. She's driving a new GMC. Mine's ten years old.

She leans across her seat and rolls down the window. I see her face through a solid sheet of water. "Hey, James," she says. "Did Cooper invite you out to his place on Saturday?"

"Yeah."

"I'm going too. Want me to pick you up?"

It's April 8. I need to start planting by the middle of the month, and I haven't got a single row laid. If the sun's out Saturday, I ought to glue my rear to the seat of a tractor. But I think about Cooper telling me to relax.

"Why not?" I say, looking through the rain at Sara Mitchell.

———

Going home, I turn off the highway at the intersection where Jackie got killed.

She was pulling into 49, and she looked right, but not left. A big truck from Sterne's Grocery Company plowed into the driver's side door. He knocked her car into a telephone pole, and for a long time afterwards, you could see a white stripe on the pole where the paint on the car had smudged off. Every time I went to town, I'd look at that pole and see that stripe of paint, and I'd feel shaky and weak, as if I'd stood too long in a hot shower and needed to lie down and cool off.

I mentioned it to three or four friends. One day I drove by and discovered the pole had been moved about fifteen feet, so that it stood on the far side of a Southern Prime billboard and was no longer visible from the intersection. I called the phone company and asked about it. They said a group of citizens had requested it be moved.

I went to one of those same folks when I found out Carol was pregnant. The whole time I was talking to him, he stared at the ground and drew circles in the dirt with his toe. When I stopped, he finally looked me in the eye.

"Well, James," he said, "the bad news is you've got a problem. The good news is you can fix it with five hundred dollars."

At first I couldn't figure out how the same man who'd gone to the phone company and demanded they move a pole just to make me feel better could say what he'd just said. Then it hit me. In both cases something needed to be moved. But having my wife get killed wasn't embarrassing, so my neighbors could lay hands on my grief and pull at least some of it aside. Having my daughter get pregnant was plenty embarrassing, so I'd have to take care of the problem this time myself.

When I get home this morning, Carol's lying on her side on the living room floor. She's got a pillow between her legs, and she's reading a biology text. Five or six months ago, I probably would have made some sort of half-assed crack about it being a little bit late to learn biology lessons, but this morning I just say, "Hi, hon."

"Hi, Daddy," she says. "There's a stack of mail on the table."

The top envelope is from the obstetrician over in Greenville. I don't have to open it to find out what's inside. It's a bill for prenatal care. There's no maternity benefit on our health insurance policy. It never occurred to me we'd need it.

"Didn't feel like going to school today?" I say.

"I just wasn't up to it."

"Not falling too far behind?"

"Not if I can help it. And Daddy?"

She's staring up at me. She's normally a thin girl, but right now her cheeks are round and flushed, and she looks so much like her mother did when she was pregnant that for a moment I feel like there's a blockage in my throat, that I'll choke if it doesn't shift aside. "Yeah, hon?"

"Everything's okay. I'm real serious."

I've been trying my best to make up for the way I behaved when I found out she was pregnant, and she's been trying her best to convince me I didn't do us lasting damage. But the truth is I was awful.

For a long time after her mother was killed, I didn't think about other women. I had my hands full being mother and father and trying to keep my farm off the auction block. I'd come home from the field every night and take over from the black woman who looked after Carol when she got in from school. I'd give Carol a bath, read her a book or two, put her to bed, then lie on the couch, drinking beer and remembering what it was like when Jackie was still alive. We used to eat supper late, sit for a while watching TV or listening to music, then we'd take a hot shower together. Afterwards, we'd walk down the hall wearing nothing but our towels and fall into bed and make love. Her hair, damp from the shower, plastered itself to my cheek as I pressed my face against hers. I could hear her labored breathing, feel her fingernails raking my back.

I passed a lot of nights just thinking about Jackie. Then one day in the Piggly Wiggly, about three or maybe four years after the wreck, I caught myself staring at the cashier. Pretty soon I was staring at every woman I found attractive, and almost every woman looked good to me. Sometimes, when I was out in the field on a tractor, I'd construct lists in my mind of everybody I wished I could sleep with. The lists got so long I started making them restrictive. I'd list all the women under thirty that appealed to me, then all the women over thirty. All the blondes, all the redheads, all the brunettes. The Baptists, the Methodists, the Presbyterians. The ones that I thought would make good mothers for Carol and the ones I thought wouldn't.

They all had one thing in common: they were married. In the Delta, almost everybody above the age of about twenty is. After a while, I just gave up and quit looking. But all those years I was raising Carol, I kept promising myself that I'd sell my land and equipment once she finished high school. I'd give her most of the money, so she could go to Ole Miss and live in a decent apartment while she got her degree, and in the meantime, I'd move to a city, Atlanta or maybe New Orleans, someplace where there'd be a few more people like me, people who weren't married and settled, people whose lives were not laid out in straight rows. If I looked hard enough and long enough, I thought, I'd find somebody to share my time with. Maybe she wouldn't make me feel the way Jackie had, but at least I'd have someone to care for.

So when Carol came home one day and sat down at the table and told me she was pregnant—and that she planned to keep the baby, even though she'd never wanted one until this one was growing inside her—what she was telling me, for all practical purposes, was to forget the promises I'd made to myself. She was telling me to get ready, at forty-four, to live the last twelve years all over again.

"You're a sweetheart," I tell her now.

She lays the biology book down and tries to sit up. She's so big she can't quite make it. I walk over and grasp her hand.

"Heave ho," I say.

With a groan she rises. "You know what?" she says.

"What, hon?"

"I'm feeling kind of funny this morning."

"Funny how?"

She rubs her stomach. "I don't know. Kind of like something's squeezing me and then letting go again."

An hour later we're at Washington Regional in Greenville. They show us into what looks like an operating room: there's an elevated table, a cart with a monitor on it, and lots of fluorescent lights that make even the air seem electric.

The doctor runs a sensor over Carol's stomach, and all of us sit gazing at a black-and-white image that appears on the monitor.

"There's your baby," he says.

It doesn't look much like a baby, it's just a shifting blob on the screen, but Carol's eyes tear up when she sees it.

In the meantime, the contractions have stopped. The doctor says he can't tell why they started, but one thing he can see from the ultrasound is that the baby's in the breech position, just like Carol was when Jackie gave birth. He doesn't need to tell me what that means. Unless the baby turns, we're headed for a C-section.

Later, while Carol's getting dressed, I follow the doctor into the hallway and ask him how much a C-section costs these days.

"Around five thousand," he says, writing something on Carol's chart, "assuming there are no complications."

Friday afternoon it clears off, so I climb onto an old red-bellied Ford and spend the rest of the day ditching. The tractor's got rice-and-cane tires on it, and they cut deep grooves across the fields. Once the water starts running off, I start to feel better. If we can just have a few clear days, we'll lay the rows out, and the seed'll be in the ground by the last week of April.

I eat supper, then go back out and work for most of the night. I fall into bed half-dead at three o'clock.

I wake up Saturday morning about nine. Sunlight is streaming through the window, and the telephone's ringing. I reach out and lift the receiver.

"Ready to go?" Sara Mitchell says.

"Damn," I say, swinging my legs out of bed, "I almost forgot."

She picks me up about a quarter till ten. I'm still feeling sleepy. I didn't drink coffee, because Cooper insists you not touch it whenever you come for a treatment, and I figure a trip to his sauna qualifies.

Sara's wearing white shorts, a tight T-shirt with a drawing of a catfish on it. Her arms and legs are as freckled as her face.

"Remember what I was telling you the other day?" she says while she drives. "About how when you farm catfish, you're not at the mercy of the elements?"

"Yeah. Changed your mind?"

"Thursday afternoon, the water in a couple of our ponds rose up over the edge of the levee. I bet we lost twenty thousand fish. They just swam away in the road ditch."

Twenty thousand fish is about twelve thousand dollars worth of stock. "If that happened to me," I say, "I don't know but what I'd swim off with them."

Sara laughs. "I might have too," she says, "if I hadn't been looking forward to coming out to Cooper's. There's not much that can beat a good three- or four-hour sweat."

Cooper's waiting for us in front of his house, which looks a lot like the picture on a bottle of Log Cabin Syrup, except that Cooper's place is huge and it's got solar panels in the roof. He and his wife built the house by hand.

This morning, he's naked except for a pair of cut-off polyester plaids. No shoes, no shirt. His chest is hairless, his arms are thin as bristles.

He says his wife is visiting their son in Yazoo City, but he's got the sauna hot and ready, so the three of us walk around back.

The structure that contains Cooper's sauna is known to all his patients as the House of Health. It's about the size of a bathhouse, and it's made out of the cypress trees Cooper felled to create space for it. There are no windows, just a single door.

Inside, he opens a cupboard and hands us each a fresh towel. It occurs to me that neither Sara nor I have brought anything to wear in the sauna. I've been here before, but it's always just been Cooper and me who got in together, and both of us just stripped off.

Which, as it turns out, is what Cooper and Sara begin to do now. He unzips his pants and lets them fall to the floor, then steps out of his boxer shorts. Sara raises her arms and starts pulling off her T-shirt.

There's an awful moment when I wonder if I'll be able to peel my eyes away. There's an even worse moment when I realize that I can't, that I'd have an easier time persuading myself to pick up a cottonmouth and kiss it.

Sara's breasts are freckled too and even larger than I would have guessed. Her nipples are not pink or rose-colored, they're brownish.

When she sees me staring at her, she says, "I've got a lump in the left one. It's malignant. Want to know what cancer feels like?"

She reaches out and grasps my right hand and pulls it toward her. While Cooper looks on, I wait to see if my palm will recoil from the breast I ached to touch a few seconds ago.

"There," she says. "Feel it?"

It's about an inch and a half to the right of her nipple. It feels like a pebble. A large one.

"It used to be damn near as big as a Ping-Pong ball," Sara says. "Cooper's been shrinking it for me."

The notion that somebody would let Cooper treat them for cancer isn't as strange to me now as it would have been a few years ago. I considered taking Carol to him for her prenatal care. But I knew she'd refuse. She thinks he's a quack.

"How long's the lump been there?" I ask.

"Almost two years," she says. "I started coming to our friend here after a regular doctor down in Jackson told me what the standard kind of treatment involved."

I ask Cooper how he's treating it.

"With a nontoxic synthetic called Cancell," he says. "It lowers the voltage in the body's electrical system. Disease cells are all low-voltage cells anyway, so when the body's voltage drops just a little bit, the sick cells die off first."

"The rest of me's doing fine," Sara says. As if to prove it, she unbuttons her shorts.

I manage to keep my eyes off her as she and Cooper enter the sauna. Quickly, I shed my own clothes and follow them.

The three of us sit together on a wooden bench, Sara between Cooper and me. Every now and then Cooper dips a big mug into a pan filled with water and then dashes the water onto the rocks. Steam rises off them, burning our noses.

Within a few minutes we're all soaking wet. The only light comes from the red-hot rods underneath the rocks, but there's enough of it for us to see one another. We're gleaming. Our skin shines under the sweat.

"I don't know," I say. "I might need some of that Cancell too."

Sara says, "What's wrong with you?"

"I feel like my voltage is running a little bit high. You saw me staring at you, didn't you?"

"I know you're by yourself, James," she says.

There are times in your life when you know you're no longer in command of your own body. The first time my back went out, I had that feeling, and I imagine Jackie must have had it in the split-second when she knew she'd been hit by something big. I suspect women feel it every time they give birth. You know some sort of force is running through you, that it may make you swoon or buck, that it may rock you like an epileptic seizure.

Maybe it's the rush of sweat from my pores, maybe the heat has gone to my head. Whatever the cause, I've got that feeling now.

"If I melt," I tell Cooper, "just throw me on the rocks. I'm feeling mighty porous."

My left knee's trembling. Sara lays her hand on it and firmly holds it still. "I'm glad I'm porous," she says.

"Yeah?"

"Yes, sir. There's some stuff inside me that needs to get the hell out."

Cooper stands up, throws more water on the rocks, and sits down next to me, so that now I'm between him and Sara.

"The body's a house, James," he says. "Houses get dirty. We're just giving ourselves a good spring cleaning."

The weather stays clear for the next two weeks. We get the rows laid out, and three days later, we start dropping seed. I own two eight-row planters that hill-drop the cotton, spray it, and fertilize it all at the same time. I've got four men working for me, so all of us together are able to keep those rigs in the field pretty much around the clock. Before too long, we'll see the cotton start growing, pushing its way up through the ground.

Carol enters her last month, and just as you'd expect, it's a trying time. She's as big as the school gym, and she hears several cracks about her size from the other kids. I tell her I intend to call a daddy or two and tell them what I think, but she says no.

"Most people are being nice about it," she says. Her homeroom teacher plans to give her a baby shower.

She's too tired to cook, so I buy us a lot of TV dinners, the fancy kind that you have to go to Greenville to buy and then hurry home with before they all thaw out. Sometimes Carol eats two of them at a sitting—sweet and sour chicken, Szechuan style, with vegetarian lasagna or Texas barbecue.

I see Sara Mitchell twice at Cooper's office and then once on the street downtown. At his office, we talk about the weather, Carol's condition, Cooper's technique, different methods of aerating catfish ponds, the possibility that the workers at Southern Prime might go on strike. We don't discuss cancer or saunas.

But the day I see her downtown, I lean on a parking meter in front of the Piggly Wiggly and say, "How's that lump?"

"Still there," she says. "It's gotten bigger again."

"How much bigger?"

"Oh, not a lot. Just a fraction of a centimeter's all."

"You don't seem to worry too much about it."

"Worrying won't cure it."

"I wish I could think like that."

"I had to learn to," she says. "Back when I first started going to Cooper, I was tied up in knots. I'm a lot more relaxed now. It feels good."

I say, "You want to come over for supper one night? Carol and I are eating some great TV dinners."

"I'll come for supper," she says, "but I won't eat a TV dinner. How about I bring a mess of fish and fry 'em up?"

She drives over the next night. She and Carol know each other by sight, because years ago, before Sara went into catfish farming, she taught PE at the elementary school, and Carol was in some of her classes.

"You've really grown up," Sara says.

"And out," says Carol.

"How you feeling?"

"Hungry."

"We can fix that."

Sara and I walk out to her truck, and I lift a heavy ice chest. She helps me tote it up onto the porch. I raise the lid and find eight or nine good-sized catfish lying on a bed of crushed ice.

"I wish they tasted like they used to," Sara says. "You remember that muddy flavor a good river cat had?"

While she and Carol work in the kitchen, rolling hush puppies and frying potatoes, I clean the fish. I clean them the way my dad did, making a single slit right behind the head, skinning them with pliers, then chopping off the head and tail and scrapping out the insides.

I hang around the kitchen drinking beer and sniffing the good smells while Sara and Carol cook the fish and mix up a big bowl of coleslaw. Watching them move back and forth between the counter and the stove, their fingers dripping batter, their faces damp and flushed, I allow myself to feel like I'm surrounded by family. I pretend it's an ordinary evening in an ordinary house, a house that's home to just the right number of bodies.

At supper Sara drinks a beer with me, and Carol drains two tall glasses of iced tea. She tells Sara what she'll name the baby if it's a girl—Jackie, after her mother—but when Sara says, "And what if it's a boy?" Carol's lips set in a determined line. She says nothing.

My fingertips whiten on the Budweiser bottle. Just last night she told me she still believed she and her boyfriend would get back together, that sooner or later he'd come home and they'd be married. "If it's a boy," I say, "she wants to name it Kenneth."

Sara chews a mouthful of catfish. "Who's Kenneth?" she says, then notices my face.

"Kenneth Bigby," I say. "He's a much-felt absence these days."

Carol lays her fork down. Her blue eyes are clear, clean of any anger. "I'm used to feeling absence," she says, looking from me to Sara. Her hands close over her belly. "Now I feel a presence for a change."

Sara nods, as if she knows what Carol means. For a moment I can't understand how she could know. Then suddenly I do understand, and understanding chills me, like cool air on your skin when you've worked up a sweat.

I don't belong at the table with these two. Nothing grows inside me.

I'm lying in Cooper's office, waiting for him to adjust me. It's the second Thursday in May. It's raining again, has been raining now for four days straight. My fields are underwater. Last night I dreamed about 1973. That spring was a lot like this spring. It poured the whole month of April, then it cleared off, and the weather turned as pretty as you ever saw it, so pretty I remember driving through the field on the tractor and singing *It ain't gonna rain, it ain't gonna snow*. I was half right. Two weeks after we got the seed in the ground, a cold front blew in, and by the time we saw the sun again, my cotton crop was just a dim memory. We managed to plant some soybeans that year, but the market was glutted. It took me two good years to make up for that bad one. This year, if I lose the cotton, I'll go under with it. I can't borrow enough to plant anything else.

Cooper makes me lie on my right side. He rolls up his shirt sleeves, he lays his hand on me. The joints in his knees and his elbows pop and crack.

While he works, I close my eyes. He's manipulating the most important bone in my body, but as always I feel nothing. And as always I find myself wishing something both unreasonable and impossible: that at least a few of the other adjustments I've had to undergo—the death of the woman I loved, the oncoming birth of somebody I'm afraid I won't care for, no matter how hard I try—could have been undergone without pain.

"Rest," Cooper says, as I lie there numb. "Just do your best to take it easy and relax. We're dealing with a large misalignment."

The next morning, Carol, Sara Mitchell, and I drive to Washington Regional in a rainstorm. Carol's due date's just ten days away, and the baby hasn't turned. The obstetrician intends to try something called external version. What that means is that while Carol lies on her back, the doctor's going to grab the baby and try to exert enough force on it to make it turn headfirst. It works about one time in three. Sometimes it brings on labor.

We pull into the outpatient lot. Sara holds an umbrella over Carol's head, and we slog through puddles toward the building.

They tell Sara and me to wait in the lobby while Carol gets ready for the procedure. We take seats in a corner. Across the room, an old man in a pair of lime-colored pajamas sits in a wheelchair, staring at a television that's bolted to a platform on the wall like one of those monitors they use to catch you stealing at the grocery store.

A middle-aged black couple sit together by the window,

whispering to each other. Their eyes are red. Either they've sat up all night or else they've been crying or maybe they've been doing both. I wonder what grief has lurched into their lives, what they had yesterday that they might not have today.

"You know what?" I say.

"What?"

"I think the word *it* is about the scariest thing in town."

She shakes her head. "No," she says, "it's not. The scariest things in town all have specific names. The word *it's* not scary till you make it scary. It might mean a good cool beer on a hot day or a thousand-dollar jackpot in the Piggly Wiggly drawing. There's no reason to assume it means a tornado or a tumor till you hear those words themselves."

"You're a good person," I say, "for me to hang around."

"I'm glad to hear it. I hope I'm available to be hung around with for many a year to come."

"When you were in about the ninth or tenth grade," I say, "did you ever have some earnest little sophomore fellow, maybe one that played tuba in the band and made *A*'s in all his French classes, come up to you in the hall between periods and clear his throat and say something really inane, like 'Sara, I wanted you to know I'm interested in you'?"

She laughs. "No," she says. "If he had, I probably would have had his pants down in about three seconds flat. I was pretty hot to trot about that time."

"What about now?"

The laugh lines disappear from her face. "Oh, my," she says.

"What?"

"Well," she says, "it's not that I'm not hot to trot."

"So what is it?"

"I should have known," she says, "that you're the sort of person that doesn't place much stock in rumors."

For a second I can't imagine what she's talking about. Then I remember the women I've seen her shooting pool with, the ones who work on her farm. They appear so swiftly in the front of my mind that I know they've been in the back all the

time. Together Sara and those women form a unit, a great big
it that I never had to name till just now.

"I guess you could say I'm trotting in a different direction
now," Sara says. "You know what I mean?"

"I guess maybe I do," I tell her. "I probably knew it all along
and just chose to ignore it. It wasn't the way I wanted things
to be."

"When your grandchild's born, James, I can't be its
grandma," she says. "But I can promise it won't ever lack
aunts."

They call me on the intercom, and we walk back to the OB
area. The nurse asks if Sara is Carol's mother, and when I say
she's not, the nurse says she's sorry, but only family can attend.

They've got Carol lying on a table in another sterile room.
There's a white web belt around her belly, and it's hooked up
to a monitor. The monitor will measure the baby's heart rate,
which is supposed to rise if the procedure brings on labor.

Carol's face is pale. She's gripping the sides of the table.

I lean over and kiss her on the cheek. "You know what you
need to do?" I say.

"Relax?"

"You bet."

The doctor tells her that there's one rule we have to agree
on. "When it hurts," he says, "it's all right to yell your head
off. Okay?"

"If she doesn't," I say, "I may."

He grins at Carol. "Dads can't stand a lot of pain."

She reaches out and squeezes my hand. "Mine can," she
says.

The doctor leans over her, and while I hold one of her hands
and the nurse holds the other, he feels around her stomach
till he finds the baby's head.

"Here we go," he says. Gritting his teeth, he pushes. Carol
gasps, and all the color that was left in her face drains away.
The doctor grunts and pushes again.

Two things happen at once. Carol shrieks, and the nurse tells the doctor he'd better look at the monitor.

He glances at it. Whatever it is he sees there makes him lock his jaw.

"Honey," he tells Carol, "your baby's not going to let me turn it. That's the bad news. The good news is you'll be a mother this morning."

A damp sheen covers her forehead. "I feel it," she says. "I really feel it."

I'm sitting on a metal stool next to Carol. They've tied her hands down to keep her from jerking, and they've given her a big shot to make her numb. I'd like to have one too, but I don't ask.

Outside, as I was waiting on them to let me into the operating room, Sara said, "Cooper claims there's never a need to do a C-section."

"Cooper's brand of medicine only works," I said, "if you really believe in it, and Carol just doesn't."

"No medicine works unless you believe in it," Sara said. "I wouldn't want a C-section if it was me, but it's not and I don't guess it ever will be. Jackie had Carol that way, didn't she?"

"Yeah. But back then the guy didn't go in and watch."

"So this is a first for you."

"The first and the last. Next time she does it, she better have a goddamn spouse."

"Sometimes," Sara said, "that's not possible," and as soon as she said it, I realized I ought to know it better than anybody else around, except maybe for Sara herself.

A couple of doctors, an intern, and two or three nurses are working away behind the curtain that separates Carol's eyes and mine from what they're doing. Metal instruments clink, I hear the sound of suction.

I sit here thinking that in a way I'm like the baby: I don't want to turn in another direction. I've clung to one notion of what a family is or should be, even though that kind of family's not possible for me. I've defined love and need in straight, narrow ways. Gentle adjustment won't work.

One of the nurses tells Carol, "It won't be much longer."

It's a different kind of medicine—maybe it qualifies as a miraculous cure. It starts inside me before I hear the baby cry, before I even hear flesh slapping flesh, before I know if the baby's made like me or made like Carol or made like something that would feel at home in one of Sara's catfish ponds. Something's growing inside me, about to burst out.

"You'll feel pressure," the nurse says. "Your baby's about to be born."

I squeeze Carol's hand, and she squeezes mine. I'm watching the top of the curtain, waiting for them to hold the baby up, but I can scarcely see. It's as if I'm looking through a sheet of rain. Tears are streaming down my face. They're salty, like sweat.

Stay-Gone Days

She'd just sacked a woman's groceries and told her to have a nice evening when she saw him. He was wearing an old surplus army jacket, faded jeans with ragged cuffs, and a pair of thick-soled work shoes. He'd shaved off his beard. He'd cut his hair, too, and it looked as if he'd recently bathed. She wondered whose bathtub he'd used, wondered if before he'd left he'd cleaned her out. Had he found the loose tile in the bathroom wall where she kept her mother's necklace, the soup bowl where she hid her grocery money?

He'd been cleaning Emmie out for almost fifteen years. She'd given him money she'd been saving for her kids' Christmas presents, money she'd set aside to pay her car insurance, her light bill, the doctor. Her husband had never noticed, and neither had anyone else, because she always recovered her losses by stealing. She checked up most evenings at the Piggly Wiggly, and the man who owned the store would never have suspected her of theft. Nobody thought she was low-down enough to steal. And the truth was she did have her ethics. She took only as much as Tom took from her, not one penny more, sometimes a lot less. She promised herself she'd pay it back one day.

For a while she'd charted his comings and goings to see if she could find any pattern. She noted his appearances on the same pocket calendars she used to keep track of her menstrual cycle: black ink for her periods, red for the days he robbed her. It was a year or two before she decided the colors should be reversed, another year or two before she understood how appropriate the original choice was. By then she'd given up trying to predict when he'd come again. He would come. Again and again.

He pulled a cart loose and strolled down the first aisle, over by the dairy section. She could see him in one of the big round mirrors her boss had attached to the wall in each corner. It was a quarter till seven, the store was empty except for him and her and two stockboys, who were in the back room, sweeping up and incinerating boxes.

She watched him pick up a block of cheese, examine it, and stick it in his jacket pocket. Then he looked over his shoulder at the mirror and waved.

It didn't take him long to do his shopping. When he rolled the cart up to the register, it held two packages of weenies, a couple of bags of potato chips, a six-pack of beer, and a jar of instant coffee.

He pulled a Milky Way out of his coat pocket, stripped the paper off, and took a bite. "I heard a good joke the other day about Jessie Jackson and a candy bar," he said. "Want to hear it?"

"No, you can just hold on till you come across somebody that appreciates stuff like that."

"It's real original."

"I bet."

He nodded at the cart. "Don't bother to ring that stuff up," he said. "You can just go ahead and sack it. It wouldn't all fit in my coat pockets."

She looked out the front window. This was a weeknight, so downtown Indianola was deserted. The store didn't do much business after six o'clock. But you never knew who might be looking at you. You never knew who was out there in the dark or what they might have in their mind.

"Why don't you just pay for it?" she said. "It's not going to cost more than about ten dollars, so you can add that amount to whatever you aim to hit me up for."

"Sweetheart, I don't have ten dollars," he said. "I had ten dollars, you think I'd be here? You think I like having to beg? From you?"

"I wouldn't exactly call what you do begging," she said.

"I'm going to act like I'm punching the register, and then I want you to act like you're handing me some money."

He stuck his hand across the counter, grabbed her wrist and held it.

"Jesus," she said, glancing first at the window and then at one of the mirrors. Any minute the stockboys would come up front and clock out.

"Hey." His features froze into that expression she often dreamed about, the one that made her wonder if he was less than flesh and blood. "You just sack this shit. You can deliver me my groceries when you get through closing up. I'm driving an old Ford Galaxy. It's parked behind the store, right down next to the bayou."

She could picture it there: a car with dented fenders, a cracked windshield, a rusty spot on the roof where the paint had peeled off. The backseat would be cluttered with beer cans, dirty underwear, a soiled pillow he'd slept on in a hundred different rest stops from here to California, from there to Maine and back. It would be parked in the shadows, near a tree or a bush, as far away as he could get from the closest source of light.

"Of course it's parked behind the store," she said. "Where the hell else would it be?"

It's 1976.

Springtime.

She's sitting next to him in Hanna Taylor's class at the Academy. The school is called an academy, but it's not military or particularly academic. It's a school for white kids whose parents have a fair amount of money. Hers don't, and neither do his. They're both here on scholarship, though their scholarships have nothing to do with scholarship. He has his scholarship because of his right arm, which can whip a football through the air seventy or eighty yards. She has hers because a group of concerned citizens believe it's an outright scandal for white girls to attend the public school with black boys. They've established a special fund. It pays the tuition for girls like her.

He wears his letter jacket to school every day, and when he gets hot and pulls it off, he's usually wearing his football jersey underneath. The jacket is red and gray, and there's a white IA stenciled onto the felt material right above his heart. There's a state championship patch on one shoulder, an all-conference patch on the other. Ole Miss would have signed him up to play football next fall, but he doesn't have the C average the SEC requires.

His hair is dark and long, the fashion of the times. He's put on weight since football season ended. It's all the senior parties, she guesses. Sometimes they have kegs. At least that's what they say.

Hanna Taylor's at her desk, looking at snapshots the editor of the school paper wants to put in this week's edition. It's supposed to be a journalism class, but it's really just an hour of daily chaos. Some people nap, their heads down on their desks. A few serious students catch up on their homework or read, and so do a few of the ones like her, the ones that are always in trouble in almost all their classes, no matter how many hours they spend with the books. Others gather in groups of two or three, leaning toward one another and whispering about something, Emmie has no idea what. Some only show up for a minute or two each day at the beginning of class. Hanna writes passes for anyone who asks, without even demanding they tell her where they're going. Everything qualifies as an assignment. A lot of people leave in their cars and come back in an hour, red-eyed and funny-smelling.

Tom leans toward her. She smells his aftershave. Old Spice, she'd bet, the same stuff her father uses. "You know Taylor's getting divorced?" he whispers.

She's always aware of him when he's there at her side, and she always hopes he'll speak to her. Every week or two he does. Most days, though, he's one of the first to disappear. She's seen him leave with several different girls.

She takes her eyes off the algebra book she's been staring at. "Yeah?" she whispers. "How come?"

He looks up the aisle at Hanna. She's thirty, short, and freckled. She has big suntanned breasts that are always on display. She wears low-cut blouses and likes to lean over when boys stand near her desk.

"You haven't heard?" Tom says.

Emmie gets tired of hearing *You haven't heard?* Sometimes she thinks people speak to her just so they can breathe that annoying question. She belongs only to the group of those who don't belong, who haven't heard, who don't even know they don't know until someone who does know points it out. She's pretty, but pretty's too little. Her clothes are wrong, her hair is wrong. She lives with her father in a rented house. Her mother left home a year ago.

"No," she says. "I haven't heard."

"Her husband caught her with Coach Carlisle."

She almost says, *Caught her doing what?* Not because she doesn't know but because she wants to hear him say it, to see what words he'd choose. She believes he'd be matter-of-fact, offhand. *Making it,* he'd say. *Getting down.*

She says, "Where'd he catch her?"

"Out behind the country club."

"In the cotton field?"

"It had soybeans planted in it last year." He looks at his watch. "You want to go smoke a joint there? I got my pickup."

Hanna writes them a pass, glancing up long enough for it to register that Emmie Fowler's finally asking, that she's leaving school with Tom Cole. She nods at Emmie, and for a moment Emmie's afraid Hanna will say something stupid to memorialize the moment—*Go for it,* maybe, or *Good for you.* Instead she says, "Emmie, you be back for your next class, okay? Don't you stay gone forever." As if Tom himself is hopeless and might as well stay gone.

The pickup is a blue GMC, a model from the late sixties. There are three or four hoes in the back, a burlap sack half-full of cotton seed, a dirty black raincoat, a football.

Once they're out of the lot, he pops a tape into the stereo, and the raspy voice of Waylon Jennings fills the cab.

"You like him?" Tom says.

"Not too much."

"How come?"

"I don't know. My daddy likes him."

"I hear he's an asshole."

"My daddy?"

He laughs. "Waylon Jennings, I meant. Actually, I hear your daddy's an asshole too."

Her father has a certain reputation. Sometimes he drinks too much at the VFW, and when he does he likes to start fights. He's not exactly George Foreman. She's seen him come home with black eyes, fat lips, torn clothes. One night last year he came home without his shoes. Whoever had beaten him up that night pulled them off him and refused to give them back.

"Who told you that?" she says.

"Hell if I know. It's just one of those things you hear."

He turns into the field behind the country club, and they bump along the turnrow. The truck's shocks groan, the hoes clatter against the tailgate.

"You ever been out here?" he says.

"No. Was I supposed to be?"

"It's one of the places folks go."

"Well, I guess I'm going here now."

"I been out here with Taylor."

"Hanna Taylor?"

"Yeah." He grins at the windshield. "And I'll tell you something, Emmie. Coach Carlisle's welcome to her."

He drives all the way to the end of the turnrow. There's a strip of woods here about a quarter of a mile wide, lots of wet undergrowth, a few swampy patches. He pulls the truck into the bushes, shuts off the engine, and shoves open his door.

"Come on," he says.

She opens her door and steps out. The ground is spongy, she feels moisture seeping into her shoes. They're her mother's shoes, a pair she left in the laundry room when she moved. Twice now she's phoned and asked for them. Emmie claims she can't find them. The shoes are plain black ones, a cheap pair her mother probably bought at Fred's or Cost-Plus, and Emmie doesn't even like them. She just wants to keep something of her mother's. When her mother left, she took something from Emmie: the knowledge that whatever else she lacked, she had two parents who lived under the same roof like everybody else's.

They walk into the woods a hundred yards or so. He reaches into his pocket and pulls out a joint. "I rolled three or four of them this morning," he says. "Smoked one in the john between first and second period."

"It's expensive, isn't it? Pot?"

"Thirty bucks an ounce."

"Where do you get the money?"

"From little girls like you. They pay me to bring 'em out to the woods and let 'em rub my muscles."

"You don't get it from girls like me. I got about seventy-five cents in my purse."

He strikes a match, cups his hands, blows a cloud of sweet smoke at her. "I'm just kidding," he says. He passes her the joint. "I work some with my daddy, and I got a couple of other things going on."

"Good for you," she says. She inhales once, coughs. "I don't have diddly going on."

"You've got some things going for you, though."

"Yeah? Like what?"

He blushes. The redness rising in his cheeks takes her by surprise. She knows she'll have to touch him, her hand is already in motion. He twists his face away, but her fingertips graze his cheek. It's stubbly. She hears static.

"I been watching you," he says, staring hard into the woods. "Lordy, I been checking up on you a long time."

"You're the only one who has."

"I guess I got the best eye."

His hands grope under her blouse. The lit joint falls from her fingers. He pushes her up against a tree, she feels the rough bark at her back, cool air on her belly, her breasts.

Then they're on the ground. It lasts a long time. She sees

his flushed face against a backdrop of branches, new green leaves, scattered fragments of the sky. She hears it happening to her, hears her hips slap the ground as he drives her.

"I want to stay here," she hears herself say. "I want to stay here forever." The noises he makes are not words.

Afterwards he crawls around on all-fours looking for the joint. "Goddamn," he says, holding it up. "It's a little bitty half-assed nub."

She's sitting on her skirt. It's dirty and damp. Her blouse is dirty too, and one button is missing. "I can't go back to school," she says. "You'll have to take me home."

"Bullshit. You're not going home today."

"Where am I going?"

"You and me'll ride."

"Ride where?"

"Where don't matter."

They drive down 49 on into Humphreys County, then he turns off onto one gravel road and then another. A couple of times he reaches across the seat and squeezes her hand. This seems like a good sign to her. The last time she had a boyfriend, way back in seventh grade, he liked to squeeze her hand too. They used to stand together behind the gym at lunch, her hand locked in his, the two of them whispering about who was and wasn't failing. Very often both of them were. Now he's failing in Texas, or at least he was the last time she heard from him, three years ago last Christmas. He moved to Houston with his parents before his eighth-grade year.

While they drive, Tom talks. He tells her he actually will go to Ole Miss, he'll just have to spend one year at MDJC, the junior college over in Moorhead. Once he gets his grades up, he'll be eligible to play in the SEC, and he assures her he'll start the first year he's in Oxford. They intend to revamp their offense for him, they'll go to a pro set to make use of his arm. She can tell he really believes everything will work out, and she envies him his optimism. Optimism is a word she knows, but optimism doesn't know Emmie.

He stops the truck in front of a crossroads store. She can tell from looking at it that it's owned and run by blacks. Posters on the porch advertise appearances by the Four Tops, Bobby Blue Bland, B. B. King, and James Brown. Royal Crown Cola, says a sign shaped like a bottletop. A Nehi thermometer hangs next to the door. There are no other trucks or cars parked out front, no trucks or cars as far as she can see.

"I'm going in and get us a six-pack," he says. "You just cool your fanny right here."

He takes a long time. She sees him through the window, he's standing at the counter, running his mouth at a middle-aged black man who sticks the beer into a paper bag, takes Tom's money, makes change and hands it back. As far as she can tell, the man never says a word.

"He was a sulky one," Tom tells her when he gets in. He pulls a beer out, pops the top and hands it to her. He opens one for himself and drinks most of it in two or three swallows. "My granddaddy," he says, cranking up, "he would've known what to do with one like that."

They ride and drink, and he tells her a story. He says that back in the fifties his grandfather on his mother's side used to own some land between Moorhead and Inverness. He raised cotton and soybeans. Two black families lived on the farm. The men drove tractors for him, the women and kids chopped cotton and picked it.

"One day," Tom says, "Grandpa went to Greenwood and bought a set of tires for Grandma's car—some automotive shop over there had a bunch of 'em on sale. He didn't have 'em put on, though, because the tires on the car were still in pretty good shape. He left 'em in his smokehouse, stacked up along the wall. Two or three days later he went out there one morning and somebody had broken the lock off and gone inside. All four of the tires were long gone."

He says his grandfather went and got his .38 and climbed in his pickup truck and drove down the road to the place where one of the black families lived—he knew one of the kids in that family had seen him unloading the tires. He tucked the pistol in his belt and walked up on the porch. He never even had to search the place. The tires were piled up right next to the window, he could see them through a gap in the curtains.

"Then listen to what happened next," Tom says. He hurls the first empty beer can out the window at a stop sign. "Grandpa went over to the door and pushed it open, and the dude was laying up in the bed with his wife, just sleeping like he had the clearest conscience in Sunflower County. Grandpa sticks the barrel in his ear and says, 'Come on, Willie B., you're going to a dance.' Willie B. opens his eyes and says, 'Please, Mr. Curtis, sir, don't shoot that gun at me. Them old bullets cost more than Willie B.'s worth.'"

Tom pounds the wheel with his palm. "Can you beat that? Grandpa thought it was so goddamn funny he didn't even take him out and scare him a little worse, which was all he aimed to do anyhow."

She doesn't laugh. She never laughs at these kinds of stories, though she often wishes they tickled her, since they seem to tickle everybody else. Her inability to find them funny is one more fence between her and the local world.

Tom fails to notice that the story didn't score. He pulls another beer out and opens it and sucks the can empty, then he opens another one and drains it quickly too. Until it gets dark, that's what they do: they ride, they drink, they smoke another joint, and he talks about himself.

She's not used to dope and beer. Her brain is full of fog, her back and legs tingle. The muscles in her face have grown lax, and her tongue feels twice its normal size. The second time he takes her it's as if it's happening to someone else, as if it's another girl lying on the truck seat, a girl who knows what to do with her legs in tight spaces, who knows what to whisper, how to move.

It's ten o'clock when they start driving again. They head back toward 49, and when they come to the crossroads where he bought his first six-pack, he stops and stares at the store. It's still open, there's a light on inside. Through the window they see the storekeeper, a woman this time. She's watching a tiny TV that stands on the counter.

Tom pulls past the store about fifty yards or so, stops the truck on the side of the road. "You know what?" he says. "I think I better grab another six." Getting out, he shrugs off his letter jacket. He's wearing nothing but a T-shirt underneath.

She says, "You'll be cold."

"No way. You've warmed me up plenty today."

Before leaving, he reaches across the seat and squeezes her knee.

She sits there thinking that sometimes it's nice to have a father who doesn't give a damn. If he gave a damn, she'd have some explaining to do. As it is she can probably just tell him good night and go to bed. He may not even notice she's been gone. Hearing a door slam, she looks out the window. Tom is running toward her through the darkness, slapping his hip and yelling.

"Richard Petty," he hollers. "Dale Unser."

When he opens the door, she sees he's wearing sunglasses. She doesn't know where they've come from or why he has them on. He jumps in and cranks up, pulls the sunglasses off. The tires heave up a hailstorm of gravel, black clouds of dust and exhaust.

"What was that about?" she says. "What did you do?"

"Had a little fun." His cheeks look green in the dashboard glow. He reaches into his right pocket and pulls out a wad of bills. "Count 'em," he says. "Time to check up."

She counts the bills quickly, stacking the ones in one pile, the fives and tens in another. "Eighty-three dollars," she says. She lays the money on the seat near his leg.

"Damn," he says. His eyes move back and forth between the road and the rearview mirror. "Tell me how they make that much money selling two or three six-packs a day and a few tubes of Afro-Sheen? They bound to have a little something nasty going on. I bet I just performed a public service."

"Why she'd give it all to you?" she says. "The storekeeper? You just go in and ask for it?"

He reaches between his legs then, and she sees the gun for the first time: sees the gleaming barrel, the cylinder, the hammer that looks about as large as her thumb.

"Wouldn't you give it to me?" he says.

It's 1976.

Springtime.

The spring that lasts forever.

At breakfast her husband always liked to read the Greenville paper. It was the Delta's only daily, and it carried lots of job ads. He worked at Modern Industries, the only factory in town. The plant was nonunion. The salaries were low, the benefits poor. He kept hoping he'd find something better, but he never complained about what he had. He'd moved to Mississippi because the factory he used to work at in Ohio had closed down, and he couldn't find work anywhere else in the state. He was almost forty now, going bald and getting a bit wide around the waist, but his appearance troubled him more than it troubled her. "I need to lose a few pounds," he'd say every week or so. She'd just smile and tell him not to worry. And for another few days he wouldn't.

"Westinghouse is opening a plant over in Greenville," he told her. He folded the paper. "They say it'll hire about two hundred folks right off, another hundred and twenty within two years. I may put in an application."

"Sounds fine to me," she said. She poured a bowlful of beaten eggs into a hot skillet. Every morning the four of them ate a whole carton. She hated washing the skillet the eggs had been cooked in, there were little white glazes you had to scrub and scrub. But she always looked forward to breakfasts with Henry and the kids. Breakfast was a time when she totaled everything up, when she reminded herself that her life, for all its red ink, had somehow ended up in the black. Only she and one other person knew how little she deserved what she had.

This morning the girls were waging a good-natured quarrel at the table about a teacher they had in common, the woman who taught math to both sixth and seventh grades.

Joanie said, "My problem with her is I think she ought to go out for football. I think she'd make a good . . . Daddy, what do they call the player that lines up on the center?"

"Noseguard," Henry said.

"She'd make a good noseguard."

"That's awful," Lynn said. She sipped the watered-down coffee Emmie gave them at breakfast. She had her mother's eyes and nose, and Joanie did too. If all you saw were their faces, they looked a lot like Emmie had looked when she was their age. But that was where the resemblance ended. Emmie made sure their clothes were up to date, and she took them to the beauty shop every few months and had their hair trimmed by somebody who knew what she was doing. "You just talk bad about Mrs. Timms," Lynn told Joanie now, "because she's tough in class."

"Momma, did you like tough teachers?" Joanie said.

"I don't think I ever had one."

"You *never* had one?"

"Well, I guess I probably had some, but maybe they just weren't tough on me."

"They liked you too much."

"No," she said, "they didn't like me much at all. They considered me dumb and hopeless."

Both girls looked at her as if they thought she was joking. Henry didn't bother looking up at all: he spread some jam onto a biscuit and said, "Of course they liked her. Can you imagine anybody not liking her?"

"I can't," Joanie said.

Lynn said, "Me neither."

Their adoration was too heavy for her to bear right now. As soon as she could, she excused herself. She went into the bathroom and sat down on the rim of the tub. She considered taking another bath. She'd taken one last night and another before breakfast, but she still felt dirty, felt like a film of filth was clinging to her skin.

Last night, when she'd walked into the parking lot behind

the store, she'd found his car right where he said it would be. He was sitting in the front seat, smoking a cigarette. She walked up to the door on the driver's side, but he wouldn't roll down his window. He gestured at the other door. She started to walk around the front of the car, then changed her mind and walked behind it.

He reached across the seat and opened the door for her. "Get in," he said.

She set the sack of stuff down on the seat and stood there. "What for? Why don't you just tell me how much you want?"

"Want's not the word. Need's the subject we're here to discuss."

She wondered what would happen if she turned and walked away. She'd asked herself that question again and again. Of all the possible answers, only one gave her comfort: he might walk out of her life forever. The others were too awful to think about.

"Okay," she said, hearing the quiver in her voice. "Let's you and me talk need. Like either one of us has the faintest notion what need is." She pushed the groceries across the seat and sat down.

He puffed on the cigarette, then stubbed it out in the ashtray. "When'd they open up the movie theatre?" he said.

"You think I know? You think I pay attention to stuff like that?"

"You got kids. I figure they like to do the normal stuff kids do, and going to a movie's one of 'em."

"My kids don't go anywhere at night."

"Yeah, well neither did I when I was their age, and neither did you either. You reckon maybe that was one of our problems?"

"I don't think too much about what *our* problems used to be. I think a lot about what my problems are today. You're the biggest one."

"I'm kind of surprised to hear you say so. I'd figure your conscience was your number-one problem and I was number two. But maybe your conscience wouldn't bother you too much if I didn't show up from time to time. Think of me as your reminder."

"You know what? You're really crazy."

His hand shot through the air so fast she scarcely saw it. He grabbed a hunk of her coat and jerked her toward him. She smelled whiskey on his breath, smelled stale sweat and cigarettes. She shut her eyes so she wouldn't have to look into his. She didn't want to see the light of waste and failure burning there.

"I've seen your house," he said. "It's little and ugly." He let go of her coat. She slumped back against the seat. "You own it, though, don't you?"

"We've got a mortgage," she said. She still hadn't opened her eyes.

"I got a mortgage too. I own a good piece of you."

"Yes," she said, "you sure God do."

He reached into the sack, pulled a beer out and opened it. She glanced at her watch: it was already seven-thirty. She would have to get away and go home.

"I'll tell you what," he said. "I got something going out west. This is the last time I'll have to ask you for anything. I'm fixing to start leaving you alone."

"You'll never do it. You may think you will, but you won't."

"It makes me feel irate when you say that."

"So feel irate. It's the truth."

"I need two thousand dollars."

"You may as well attach six zeroes," she said. "I couldn't come up with that if I pawned everything I owned."

"There's a safe in the store. I saw it in the office."

"I don't have a key to it."

"It's a combination safe. And you know the combination, don't you?"

She didn't answer.

"Of course you do," he said. "You just take the money out. You're the last one to leave a lot of nights. Tell everybody some mean-assed fellow barged in at closing time and stuck a gun in your face. It could happen."

"I know it could."

"The owner trusts you," he went on, "and the cops will too. Hell, everybody trusts Emmie. She only got one or two lines next to her name in the Academy yearbook, because she was one of those girls nobody paid much mind to except for one guy that went a little wild for her tits, but Emmie, she's as honest as they come. She's not one to sneak and cheat."

He leaned toward her and ran his palm along her cheek. "You used to be something," he said. "Now I bet you're something else."

"No," she said, "I'm nothing."

"That's a damn lie, honey," he whispered. He'd begun to nuzzle her neck. She sat there rigid, scared to say stop, afraid that if she did he'd send her home with a busted nose. She didn't fear the pain itself, it was the having to explain that scared her.

"I'll tell you what you are," he said, nipping at her ear. "You're a husband, two kids, a house, and a reputation. I don't need that money for a couple of days, but I can't wait any longer than that."

When he let her out, she drove home and took her bath. Now, sitting on the edge of the tub, she rejected the notion of taking yet another one. It wouldn't do what the first two hadn't. It wouldn't make her feel clean.

She dropped the girls off at school, then stopped by the post office to pick up the store's mail. After that, she drove down the street to the Piggly Wiggly and parked in front of it. Employees weren't supposed to park out front, but her boss wouldn't say a word to her about it if he happened to notice her car. He'd figure she had a good reason, and he'd be right. She didn't want Tom to catch her behind the store by herself.

What she'd told him last night was the truth: there was no way in the world she could get two thousand dollars, unless she really did take money from the safe and walk outside and hand it to him. If she did that, she might as well just keep on walking down the street to the police station and turn herself in. Covering up a hundred here and there was one thing.

This was altogether something else. Even if she got away with it the first time, sooner or later he'd try to hit her hard again, and she wouldn't fool anybody then.

She spent the day as she always did. She phoned in orders to the warehouse, she walked the aisles and checked the shelves to make sure everything was fronted, she did her stint at the register, sacking groceries and urging everyone to have a nice day. All the while she kept waiting for him to walk in. Last night he'd administered the injection, today he'd stop by to witness the serum's effects.

He didn't come. And the more she thought about it, the more it made sense that he wouldn't. He'd let the poison have time to travel through her, he'd wait till he could cut her and draw something besides blood. He'd wait till she was empty of herself.

She finished checking up, and she carried the leather satchel with the day's receipts next door to the bank and put it in the after hours depository. Then she started walking toward her car, but her legs wouldn't stop when they got there. She walked on down the street, past the drug store and the newspaper office, past the hardware and the Methodist Church.

When she walked into the station, she saw a bunch of stolen street signs propped against the wall, two or three stolen bikes, and a pair of muddy shoes. Each item wore a tag, with the date it had been recovered printed on it. The waiting room was otherwise empty. She went up to the dispatcher's window and asked to see the chief.

He was standing in the hallway, getting ready to go home. She knew him, he and his wife shopped at the store. He was the first black chief the town had ever had.

"Hi, Emmie," he said, one thumb locked around a belt loop. "What you up to this evening?"

"I need to talk to you."

"Anything wrong at the store?"

"No," she said. "But there's something wrong with me. Something's been wrong a long time."

———

They start leaving school together every day during Hanna Taylor's class. Most days they drive out into the woods and smoke a joint, and he makes love to her, and then they go back. They hang around together in the hallways between periods, standing close to each other and whispering. They sit together at lunch and always at the same table, the one directly underneath the basketball goal.

But some days when they leave school, they just stay gone. They ride the highways from one end of the Delta to the other, they ride the back roads too. Once they ride as far south as Jackson. Another time they even cross the river.

They call these days the stay-gone days. On stay-gone days they drink a lot of beer and smoke a lot of dope and make love three or four times. They do it on the ground, in the back of the pickup. They do it in seedy motels in towns like Anguilla, Tutwiler, Lake Village, places where you can rent a room for eight dollars, where they never check ID's or demand your license plate number. They do it once on top of the levee.

"You're something," he tells her while his hands roam her body. "I'd climb an oak to get to you."

The next day they drink a six-pack and smoke two joints, and she shimmies up a tree and makes him prove it.

She goes to school less and less, but her grades actually improve. At first this puzzles her. With all the drinking and smoking she's been doing, her mind should be anything but clear, yet it seems clearer than it's ever been before. After a while she thinks she knows why. What she gets from Tom is the main thing she's lacked. It's called attention, and it's given her a little bit of faith in herself, a little bit of faith that she matters. He's opened her up. What's outside has started pouring in. She makes a C+ on a biology test, a B- in algebra. She pulls a straight B in world history.

She notices things now she's never noticed before. The floor tiles in her bedroom are all beige, except for one green one near the baseboard. The clock on the front of the bank doesn't work. There's a faint white scar on Hanna Taylor's chin, and

Coach Carlisle's left eye wanders.

She also notices things about the stores Tom robs. They're always at least twenty miles from Indianola, usually more, and they're always outside Sunflower County. They're always in the country. They're always small, usually run-down, and there's never a dog around. Black people always run them.

He robs them at night. If it's a cool night and he's wearing his letter jacket, he pulls it off before he goes in. Sometimes he puts on the black raincoat that he carries in the back of the truck. He keeps the shades in his pocket and sets them on his nose as he nears the door. He keeps the pistol tucked under his belt.

He never tells her when he's going to hit a place, but she knows anyway. He talks a lot before he does it, talks for hours, telling her how he aims to burn up the SEC, how it won't be long before she sees him on television. He starts drinking beer at a crazy pace, popping one can after another. She's amazed he can still drive. She seriously doubts whether or not he could get out of the store alive if anybody ever offered resistance. He's already admitted he'd never use the gun, he'd run if someone challenged him.

One night they're driving around up in Quitman County, and he's running his mouth and draining Bud cans as fast as she can hand them to him. She says, "You already picked the place out?"

He laughs. "You mean I'm getting predictable?"

"You are to me."

"Long as I'm not to them."

"Somebody's liable to shoot you one night. They're liable to pull a shotgun out from under the counter and use you to add some color to the place."

"Would you ache?" he says. "If I became a mural on the wall?"

"I'd flat-out die," she says. She means it. She can't imagine living like she used to, and she can't imagine she'd want to be with anyone else or that anyone else would ever come along. She and Tom haven't talked about what'll happen next month after graduation, but she intends to enroll at the junior college too. She'll get a job in a store, take one or two courses, and see as much of him as their schedules permit.

"It'll never happen," he says.

"You don't know."

"I do too. Imagine you're Lee Roy or Essie Mae or whoever. Would you risk getting shot trying to keep a white boy from making off with fifty dollars? When you know that even if you shoot him before he shoots you, you got a white sheriff to deal with, then a white judge and a mostly white jury?"

"Times have changed," she says.

"Not that much."

"So that's why you always rob black folks?"

"That's one reason."

"What's the other?"

His chest swells noticeably beneath the letter jacket. "Hell, white folks know me," he says. "They've seen me play ball against their teams."

He drinks two or three more beers, then turns onto a gravel road they drove down earlier today. It's narrow. Mounds of dirt lie in the ruts where tractor tires have slung mud. Off to the right, in somebody's field, she sees a set of running lights.

It's been a cool spring, and this is a cool night. She's got her window rolled up. David Allen Coe is singing on the stereo. It's a song about a guy who's come back from the war, and he's thinking about a German girl, his pretty fraulein, who he left on the banks of the old river Rhine. She shuts her eyes and imagines the German girl. She sees her walking down the street in some little German town. Her country is in ruins and so is she. An ocean lies between her and what she needs, he's left and she knows he won't be back.

Tom stops the truck. Opening her eyes, she sees the store through the windshield, through the paste of splattered insects and field dust. It's about sixty yards away. It looks like it was once a tenant shack. It's built two or three feet off the ground, it's got a tin roof, a sagging porch. There's a light pole in front of it, a single bulb burning, insects swarming in the glow. A gas pump is standing in the store yard too, but Johnson grass has grown up around it. Inside there's probably just a soft drink box with Cokes and beer floating in water that by now is up to room temperature. There'll be a candy counter too, and it'll have a glass front, so you can see the M&Ms, Hershey bars, Milky Ways, and Crackerjacks. A plastic cookie jar will be standing on top of it, and next to the cookie jar there'll be a jar of dill pickles. The cash register will be nearby, on top of another counter, and God only knows what's underneath.

She shivers. "I wish you'd quit this," she says.

"Beer and dope's not free."

"Maybe we should just get jobs."

"This is the line of work that suits me. This and throwing footballs."

He turns the truck around, puts it in park and opens the door. He reaches under the end of the seat and takes out the pistol. It's a .38, he's told her, the same one his grandfather once pointed at the man named Willie B.

"I been in there before," he says. "It's run by a dude that's about seventy years old. I'll be back in a minute and a half."

He pulls off the letter jacket and shoves it behind the seat. Looking through the back glass, watching him start off toward the store, she's struck by the feeling that something's not right. She tries to think what it could be. He's got the dark glasses, she saw him pick them up. He's got the pistol. He took off the letter jacket.

He enters the ring of light, walks past the gasoline pump. It's then that she notices the white jersey.

It's the one the team wears in road games. It's got a big red 7 on the front and the back, a conference championship patch on each shoulder. His name is stenciled on the back in red letters. He's forgotten to put the raincoat on over it.

For three or four crucial seconds she freezes. Then she releases the door latch and jumps out. He's on the porch, opening the door with one hand, holding the pistol in the other.

She intends to yell his name, but what comes out is a whisper. Running toward the store, she tries again, with the same result.

She's at the foot of the steps when he steps out the door. He's holding a few bills in one hand. "What?" he says, the color draining from his face.

"The jersey," she says, trying this time to whisper, but what comes out now is a yell. "It's got your damn name on it."

In that instant she sees him for the first time as he is. His cheeks go slack, his hands begin to tremble. The sunglasses look from her to the door, then back at her again. He takes a step toward her, then stops. She knows without being told that this is what happens when he has to take a test. He can't commit himself to an answer. If he held a football in his hand instead of a .38, he would have reached a decision a long time ago. He was made for something less than real life.

He won't pass his courses at MDJC, he'll never play ball for Ole Miss. He'll never keep a steady job or own a house, though she suspects he'll break into a few. If he fathers a child, the child will never know him, and the child will be the fortunate one.

When he makes up his mind, nobody can stop him. She tries: she calls his name again, but he's already turning. He pulls open the door, and his right hand explodes.

This is what she said as he sat there across the desk, his dark face impassive, a pen in his hand, several sheets on the legal pad already filled with facts that would separate her from everyone she loved:

He came the first time when we were just closing. I hadn't seen him for three years. I was twenty-one. I'd been married to Henry for a year and a half. Joanie was a baby. She had jaundice.

He followed me out to my car. I'd parked it out back like we were told. It was February. It had just snowed. He wasn't wearing a coat, just a flannel shirt. I'm cold, he said. He hugged himself like he thought he had to prove it. I said Why don't you wear your letter jacket? He told me he'd sold it.

He said Things have worked out real well for you. He said I wish things had worked out like that for me too. He said I'm not sure you deserve it, but then nobody does.

He asked me to loan him a hundred dollars. I said no. He said You know, I could make you awful unhappy. I could tell your husband stuff he wouldn't want to know. It's all stuff you may have forgotten.

But I hadn't forgotten any of it then, and I haven't forgotten it now. I remember what I saw when I looked in the door of that little country store. The man must have come out from behind the counter. He was lying stretched out on the floor. He was wearing old khakis, a dingy shirt, and a pair of suspenders. But the thing that caught my eye was his spectacles. They were lying on the counter next to the cash register. The lenses were half an inch thick. I wondered if he'd had them on when Tom walked in. I wondered if he'd seen those red letters.

On the way home Tom said What are you sniffling about? He said If you don't shut up I may hit you. He said He was just an old man and just a nigger at that.

And I said What are we? What are we just?

*M*ississippi *History*

For a while my closest friend at the Academy was a kid named Chuck Sterne. Like all the students there, we had transferred from other schools. Chuck had come across town from Indianola Junior High, and I'd come in from one of the county schools. We hit it off so well because neither of us played football and we both made good grades and were interested in history, particularly the Civil War.

The first time Chuck's father phoned and asked me to spend the night, I was sitting in the living room reading. It was fall, and my dad had just come in from the field. Little shreds of cotton clung to his work clothes. He smelled of dust, sweat, and defoliant. The phone rang just as he came in, and I heard him answer it.

Then he said, "Sure. It's fine with me. Yeah, he's right here."

Dad handed me the phone and stood there while I talked to Mr. Sterne.

After I hung up, Dad said, "I didn't know you knew Joel Sterne's boy."

It was typical of my father not to know who my friends were. He spent most of his life on a tractor, and I know now that when he wasn't on the tractor, he was busy worrying about losing the tractor and the land he plowed with it and the house he and my mother and I lived in.

I said, "Chuck and I have classes together."

"You know his dad's president of Sterne Grocery Company?"

"Yes, sir. He's on the board of directors at the Academy too."

"You'll see an awful nice house Friday night."

"I've already seen it from the street."

"Well, seeing it from the inside'll be different. Anyhow, what were you doing in that part of Indianola?"

"Mother drives through there sometimes when she's bringing me home from school."

"Little bit out of the way, I'd say."

"She likes to look at the houses."

Dad beat dust from his khakis. He said, "Thank God looking don't cost."

The Academy had opened three years earlier, in 1967, when everybody realized integration couldn't be avoided much longer. At that time it served grades one through five, and classes met at the Methodist Church. But now it offered instruction to all twelve grades, and we had a new brick building out behind the Skate-a-Rama. The football team was called the Rebels. The school colors were red and gray, the school mascot was a skinny, old Confederate officer with a long white beard. At football games everybody waved a Confederate flag, and the band played "Dixie" after every first down.

My favorite teacher that year was Coach Clayton. He was a tall man, well built, with red hair and greenish-brown eyes. He'd played football at Ole Miss. Now he coached running backs and taught Mississippi History—normally you had to be in ninth grade to take that class, but the principal had let Chuck and me sign up a year early. I liked Clayton so much because he never gave me a hard time about not playing football, and he knew his subject well, and in the classroom he put on quite a show. He could tell you the name of every current member of the state legislature, plus the county each one came from and his party affiliation. He knew the birthdate and birthplace of every governor and lieutenant governor of Mississippi and—this impressed us most—the land area, in square miles, of every single county in the state.

The day I went to Chuck's house for the first time, Clayton began class like he usually did, with a funny story. Sometimes the stories concerned the misfortunes of the Mississippi State

Bulldogs, but more often than not they poked fun at black people.

"Back when I was in high school," Clayton said, perched on the edge of his desk, "there was an old colored guy who worked at Hewitt's Furniture Store in Greenville. This fellow could really play the guitar.

"Well, one night some of my friends and I were at a high school dance and the band was bad, so we decided we'd go get Son—Son Johnson was his name—and bring him back and let him show the band how to play. We drove over to the Ebony Club, where we knew he liked to hang around, but they said he hadn't been there that night. So we asked where Son lived, and somebody gave us an address.

"Turned out it was a neat little shack down close to the levee. We went up and knocked on the door, and after a while an old colored woman opened it. I told her we were looking for Son Johnson, and she said Son wasn't there. So I said, 'Well, can you tell us where to find him?' And she says, 'He at the hospital.' I asked her what was the matter with him, and she said he'd been stabbed. 'Stabbed?' I said. 'Who in the world did that?' And she grinned at me and said, 'He *say* I did.'"

Walking to Chuck's house that afternoon, we discussed the battle of Vicksburg, wondering if John C. Pemberton, who'd been born in the North, hadn't purposely let Grant and Sherman tunnel under his fortifications. But every few blocks, without warning, one of us would suddenly holler *"He say I did!"* Then both of us would slap our thighs and howl.

Chuck's house really was awfully nice inside. You could see yourself in the hardwood floors. There were chandeliers in every room, lots of dark cabinets filled with crystal and china, and in the living room, two rosewood rockers that Chuck said had once graced the veranda at Beauvoir, Jeff Davis's home.

Chuck's parents were divorced, so there was no one at dinner except the two of us and Mr. Sterne. He was short like Chuck and dark haired and probably about thirty-eight or forty. He drank bourbon on ice with his meal.

After dinner the three of us sat around a fire in the den. Chuck told his dad Coach Clayton's story about the black man who played the guitar, and Mr. Sterne laughed along with us at the punch line. He seemed to enjoy our company; he was in a happy, talkative mood.

We eventually got off on to the Civil War. He said, "Have you toured any of the battlefields, Kenny?"

"Shiloh," I said, "and Vicksburg. And Fort Pemberton, if you count that. Plus I've been to the Old Capitol."

He said, "Shiloh's probably my favorite. It's such a quiet place, so still—which is how it ought to be when you think how much suffering and dying went on there." He talked about other battlefields he and Chuck had visited— Fredricksburg, Antietam, Bull Run—and he described each one so vividly that for a few moments I believed I'd seen them all.

On the way up to bed, he said he'd like to show me his library. He led Chuck and me into a room at the end of the hall and turned on the lights. There were a lot of tall book-cases in the room, all of them full. He pointed at one and said, "That's my Civil War section."

He owned all of Bruce Catton's books. I'd read the first two volumes of Catton's trilogy, but the town library didn't have the third. I asked if I could borrow it. He handed it to me and said, "Catton's good, but when you get through with him, you ought to read Shelby Foote. He's the best, as far as I'm concerned."

As I turned to go, I saw a black-and-white photo hanging on the wall. The picture was hard to decipher. Two black bars formed a twisted arch; in the space between the two bars, black letters spelled out an inscription, but you couldn't tell exactly what the letters said because there were trees in the background, dark like the letters themselves. Though I didn't know it then, I would one day stand exactly where the pho-tographer had stood and take a black-and-white snapshot of my own. And those trees would muddle the message in my photo too.

"*Arbeit macht frei,*" Mr. Sterne whispered. "That's German, Kenny."

"What does it mean?"

"It means *work will make you free.* But it didn't, not for anybody who walked under that arch. That's a picture I took of a concentration camp."

Chuck said, "My mother's father died there."

Mr. Sterne asked me if I knew about the Holocaust.

"I've heard the word," I said, "but I'm not sure what it means."

He switched off the light. "Maybe when you finish Bruce Catton and Shelby Foote," he said, "you'll be interested in looking into it."

I visited Chuck often. I spent several Friday nights with him, and sometimes, on weekdays, I'd walk home with him and stay at his place until supper, when my mother picked me up.

We talked about one day writing a book together. We were hazy on exactly what the subject would be, but it would most likely concern the Civil War. Maybe we would write about John Singleton Mosby, the fabled Gray Ghost. Kicked out of college for killing another student, he'd learned the law in prison, and when they let him go, he became an attorney and later on a guerrilla.

Or maybe we would write a mean book about Grant. He was a drunkard, Chuck and I agreed, and anyway he had once done something nasty to one of Chuck's relatives, a great-great-grandfather on his dad's side of the family. The grandfather had applied for a permit to trade cotton in Memphis in 1862, when Grant was commander of the Army of the Tennessee, and Grant had not only refused, he'd run him out of town and even threatened his life.

Chuck said we could decide what to write about in college. He planned to major in history at Ole Miss, and I said I would, too, though privately I had doubts that I'd be going. It cost more than five hundred dollars a year to send me to the Academy, and I knew it was about to break my father. College could only cost more.

Chuck was trying to teach me to play chess. "I can't play with Dad," he said one day as he unfolded a hand-carved board his father had bought him. "He'd either have to beat me in nothing flat or pretend, and he says both would be bad."

"Your dad's an interesting guy."

Chuck was setting up the pieces. "He's smart," he said, "and he's a real good businessman too. We're supplying independent grocery stores in four states, and we're going to start doing business in Alabama next year. Dad's not too happy, though."

"How come?"

"He misses my mother a lot."

"Why did she leave?"

"He told me it was because even though she loved us, she loved somebody else more. It was pretty awful when it happened. I still love her and everything, but sometimes I'm kind of glad she's gone."

"Really?"

"She and Dad fought a lot and it usually ended up with him crying. I always hated that. But I guess probably he'd be happier if she came back."

"Is there any chance she will?"

"I don't think so. He used to call her fairly often, but he'd always end up screaming into the phone, really nasty stuff, too."

"What were they fighting about?"

"I never could figure that out."

"He won't tell you?"

"I don't ask."

"Well, I like your dad," I said, and as I said it I thought how nice it would be to have a father who'd made a lot of money, who owned a lot of books and had traveled all over the world.

———

I never did learn to play chess. But I learned a lot of other lessons from Chuck and Mr. Sterne.

One night the three of us sat down together in the den, and Mr. Sterne showed me a pamphlet he'd picked up a few years earlier, when he visited the concentration camp at Auschwitz. I saw a picture of Block Eleven—"the Block of Death," he said—and another picture of the courtyard outside it, where twenty thousand prisoners were executed. I saw the double-barbwire fence, which had been hooked up to a massive electric generator.

"Sooner or later, most of the prisoners lost hope," Mr. Sterne said. "And a lot of them—nobody knows exactly how many—a lot of them threw themselves against that fence."

"We think that's how my mother's father died," Chuck said.

"But we don't know for sure," his dad said. "That was one of the worst things about those camps, Kenny. When you went there, they tattooed a number on your arm, and your name no longer mattered. When you died, they incinerated your remains."

He tried to explain what the Holocaust was all about. He said Hitler had hated the Jews because they were different. He'd tried to kill them all and had almost succeeded.

I remember how troubled I felt that night lying in bed beside Chuck. He and his father were Jews—that much I understood—but I did not understand how that made them different. They looked like I did, they talked like I did, they dressed like I did. The only real difference in them and me, as far as I could see, was that they were rich and I wasn't.

The next afternoon, I went to the field with my father. He was scrap picking—it was early November—and he needed me to tromp the cotton down after he dumped it in the trailer. When we'd finished, I rode with him to the gin. On the way I asked him why some people didn't like Jews.

He began to knead his left eyebrow with his index finger, which was what he did whenever you asked him a tough question.

Finally, he said, "I guess the truth is, a lot of folks are jealous of them."

"Why?"

"Well, a lot of them have made a good bit of money."

"Did they make it dishonestly?"

"Some of them probably did. But you could say the same thing about any other group of folks that made money. Look, son, this business of not liking Jews, it's mostly just stupidity," he said. "A fellow like your friend's father, he does a lot of good. He must employ five, six hundred people out at the grocery company, not to mention all the truck-driving jobs he creates. I know a lot of folks that work for him, and I never heard any of them say he'd treated them unfair. I don't know if you know this or not, but he donated the land the Academy's built on. He could've made a lot of money by selling it, but he chose not to. There's several Jews in business in Indianola, and in general, they're good folks. I don't give a shit if they eat special pickles."

On Christmas Eve morning, Mother and I drove into town to pick up a glazed ham at the Piggly Wiggly. The streets wore their usual decorations. An eight-foot peppermint candy cane hung from the clock on the front of the bank, and a banner spanning Front Street said MERRY CHRISTMAS. A life-size Santa rotated in the Piggly Wiggly window.

Going into the store, Mother dropped a quarter into Mr. Willis's tin cup. Mr. Willis, who was blind, always sat near the door, singing and playing an archtop guitar. This morning's song was "My Son Calls Another Man Daddy." Mr. Willis did not traffic in holiday cheer.

Indianola had once seemed huge, but lately I had the feeling it was shrinking, that there was half of what there'd once been. Take the water fountains here in the store. Once there had been two—one painted white, one painted black—and everybody knew which one to drink from. Now only the white one remained, and as best I could tell, nobody drank from it. I had been told not to. There used to be two waiting rooms at

Martin Brothers' Clinic. One had overstuffed couches, pad-
ded chairs, lots of magazines, and a big color TV. The other
room just had benches. These days there was only one room.
The chairs were plastic and uncomfortable. The magazines
were gone. The TV had been removed. And no one ever came
early, like everybody used to, to sit around and talk.

Mother paid for the ham. I toted it out to the car and laid it
in the backseat. Then Mother walked around behind the car
and unlocked the trunk.

She lifted out a grocery sack. "I've got something I need
you to do for me," she said. "Will you do it?"

"Sure," I said. Only my mother or my father or Chuck Sterne
could have gotten that answer from me without first telling
me what the it was.

"Good," she said. She handed me the sack and told me to
get into the car.

She cranked up. I peered into the sack. I saw ten or twelve
oranges, a few apples, a plastic bag filled with pecans. Also, a
container of Folgers coffee and a small doll. The doll wore a
pink dress. She had chocolate-colored skin and frizzy black
hair.

Mother drove across the railroad tracks and turned left. The
change was immediate and stark. The street was full of pot-
holes. The houses were mostly little shotgun dwellings with
sagging roofs; tin siding was tacked onto the walls to cover
chinks. The yards were small and muddy, the dogs skinny
and mean looking.

Mother made a left onto a narrow street that turned into a
dirt lane after about fifty yards. The houses here looked even
worse than those on the previous street. She stopped the car
before one of the houses but left the motor running.

She said, "You remember those colored folks who used to
work for your dad? The ones he let go last summer?"

Dad had driven into town one morning in August to try to
get a loan from the bank. My tuition was due, I think, and I
suppose he didn't have it. Apparently the bank let him have
the loan, but he came home with a red face, and when he got

out of his pickup truck, he slammed the door so hard I thought it would fall off. He was silent all the way through lunch; afterwards, instead of asking me to go to the field with him, he just got up and walked out, letting the screen door crash against the facing.

Sometime that afternoon he fired a black man named Robert Harris. I heard him tell Mother he'd been driving by the field down on the back side of our place when he saw the John Deere standing idle on the turnrow. He parked the truck and jumped the drainage ditch and was just in time to see Robert hop up off the ground, wiping sleep out of his eyes. Robert was married and had several kids, and he'd worked for Dad and lived on our place for five years. I'd heard Dad say he was the best help he'd ever had. But that day he told him he wanted him and his family gone by tomorrow night at the latest.

I told Mother that I remembered them. She said, "They're staying in this house now. Just take the sack up there and give it to whoever opens the door."

I got out of the car and walked across the yard. The front steps creaked as I climbed them. A board was missing from the porch, and those that remained were in a state of dry rot. I could smell woodsmoke.

I knocked on the door. Behind the window nearby, curtains parted. A pair of eyes stared at me. Then the curtains fell together again.

A woman I recognized as Robert's wife opened the door. A little girl stood behind her, clinging to her leg.

I offered the woman the sack. "My mother asked me to bring this," I said.

She looked over my shoulder at the car. Then back at me.

"Take that away from here," she said.

"It's just some stuff for your kids. Some apples and oranges and stuff."

"Take it on home."

I was confused and—I know now—angry too. I reached into the sack and pulled out the doll. "At least take this. For your little girl."

The little girl let out a high-pitched keen, a drawn-out "Please!" The woman's mouth collapsed at the corners. She reached out and snatched the doll. She shoved it in the little girl's face. "Take it, goddamn." The little girl squealed, grabbed the doll, and ran off.

The woman and I stood there face-to-face. I almost hugged her. I almost said "I'm sorry," though I didn't know exactly what I was sorry for. Later it seemed to me that I almost did a thousand things, that a world of possibilities occurred to me in that instant and I rejected all but one.

I set the sack down on the porch and told her Merry Christmas.

One morning Coach Clayton walked into our Mississippi History class laughing. Chuck and I looked at each other and grinned. We knew a funny tale was on the way.

"I was just filling up my car at the Gulf station," Clayton said, "and the attendant told me a neat little story. Seems that one day this rich New York couple named Goldberg found a little colored baby lying in a basket on their doorstep. The Goldbergs were good-hearted folks, so they took the colored baby in and raised him as if he were their own.

"Well, one day the boy turned twenty-one, and the Goldbergs sat him down and told him he wasn't their natural son, that they'd found him on their doorstep, and as they told him the story, they watched his face to see if he was getting upset at the news.

"But he didn't look upset at all. In fact, he broke out in a big toothy grin. And when they finished, he said, 'So that explains it. All my life, whenever I wanted something from a department store, I'd have these two different urges. One was to steal it, and the other was to try to haggle the cashier down. And since I could never choose between the two, I just paid the sticker price, like everybody else.'"

I don't know how many people laughed. Probably most of the students did, though I doubt that very many of them understood more than half the joke. In any case, my ears were deaf to every noise except the cackle that emerged from my mouth. Chuck's mouth was open too. He stared at me but didn't make a sound.

The collar of my shirt was soaked when class ended. Chuck grabbed his books and hurried out the door. I caught up with him out on the sidewalk.

"Hey," I said. "I was just laughing out of habit."

"I can't believe you did that. My father showed you all those pictures and told you what had happened to our people, and you laugh like a jackass at a stupid story like that."

"We always laugh at his stories."

"Most of them are funny. This one wasn't."

"Some of the others wouldn't be funny either," I said, "if you were black."

"I'm not black."

"They don't go to school here," I said. "If they could go to school here, he wouldn't get to tell those other stories."

"You're right," Chuck said. "They don't go to school here. And you know what?" He walked up close to me, as if he didn't want any of the other kids milling about nearby to hear what he intended to say. "If you're not careful, you may not be here next year either. Your dad pays your tuition in installments. You have to make special arrangements for that. And my father's on the board of directors."

The next morning, when I entered Coach Clayton's classroom, Chuck was sitting all the way across the room from our normal spot. He didn't look at me, just kept his eyes on his textbook.

Usually, Clayton was in the room early, chatting with the students, but that morning his desk was empty. Just as I'd decided that Mr. Sterne had probably ordered him fired, Clayton walked in. He was whistling.

He laid his textbook down on the edge of his desk and faced the class. "I said some things yesterday I shouldn't have," he told us. "That joke I told about the folks who found the baby?

It wasn't very funny. I'm sorry I told it. Mississippi History's serious business."

He picked up the textbook and opened it. I cleared my throat and raised my hand.

"Yeah, Kenny?" Clayton said.

I was watching Chuck. I thought I saw him flinch when Clayton said my name, but I wasn't sure then, and I'm not sure now. Maybe he didn't suspect what was coming. Maybe, despite the way I'd laughed at Clayton's joke, Chuck Sterne still trusted me.

"I don't quite understand," I said. "Why wasn't the joke funny?"

Clayton was a history teacher, not a mathematician; but I had the impression he was performing some quick calculations. What were the odds he could give an honest answer and still retain his job next fall?

He must have decided the odds weren't too good. "It just wasn't funny," he said and started flipping pages.

"I guess I thought it was," I said. "I mean, I thought it was about as funny as that story you told us about Son Johnson— the guy whose wife stabbed him and said *He say I did?*"

Clayton was fair skinned: he had probably turned red. I don't know; I was gazing at Chuck, who stared at his textbook as if he'd like to disappear into its pages.

I said, "Did somebody here complain about the joke?"

Clayton said, "Drop it, Kenny."

A whine had crept into my voice. It disgusted me and, at the same time, made me feel more combative. I had nothing at my disposal except angry words and nasty gestures.

"If somebody complained about it," I said, "I'd like to know who. And why."

This time Clayton sounded like a coach. "Knock it off. Shut up."

He must have looked at my face then. His voice softened.

"It wasn't very smart of me to tell that joke, Kenny, " he said. "And you're not being very smart now."

———

One day, about a week later, Mr. Sterne phoned me at home.

"Chuck told me what happened between you two," he said, "and I want you kids to bury the hatchet. You're both fine boys, and I consider you my friend. I think Chuck's got something he wants to say."

So Chuck came on the line and told me he was sorry, and I said I was, too, and we promised to renew our friendship.

We started sitting next to each other again in Mississippi History. I even went over to his house once or twice. We carried it off as well as we could, but of course it wasn't the same.

Summer came, affording a natural boundary. The next fall we had no classes in common. We saw each other in the corridors from time to time, and we were always polite; we would even stop and chat.

One of those encounters is preserved for the historical record in the 1973 Academy yearbook. It's a wide-angle shot of a hallway between periods. You can see Colonel Rebel in a mural on the wall—he's dribbling a basketball. You can see several kids peering into their lockers, pulling books out or shoving them in. You can see Coach Clayton pushing open the door to the men's room. And in the foreground, you can see Chuck Sterne and me. We're about the same size. We both have blue eyes. His hair, like mine, has lapped over his collar. We're both wearing khakis and pullover shirts.

We're grinning at each other, discussing something inconsequential.

Hungarian Stew

Malina is dreaming about a particular bench in Lazienki Park, a bench where she often sits and reads on warm summer afternoons while Petita, her cocker spaniel, prowls the pathways, looking for an unsuspecting cat. She's been going to that bench for more than fifteen years. The first time she went there she was a student new to Warsaw—thrilled to live in the city of Chopin and Prus, pleased to be away from her parents and her grandmother. The last time she sat on the bench she had just left the Hotel Victoria, where the airline has its offices, and there was a round-trip ticket to the U.S. in her purse. She stayed a long time that day, wondering if she would ever see Lazienki again, wondering if a year from now she'd want to.

Suddenly she feels a finger poking her in the ribs.

"Hey," Jack says. "Wake up. You're about to miss Delta Implement Company."

There's bluegrass on the car stereo, a fast song Jack loves: "Foggy Mountain Breakdown" or maybe it's "Rocky Top." A shower of banjo notes washes over her.

She sits up and looks out the window. Through the darkness she can see a bunch of tractors rowed up in a lot beside the highway.

She rubs her eyes. "What time is it?"

"Ten till one. Welcome to Indianola, Mississippi, home of B. B. King and me."

She and Jack have driven straight through from western Virginia. She thinks she fell asleep in Memphis.

Driving through town she sees a McDonald's, a Kentucky Fried Chicken, something called Mr. Quik that looks a lot like

57

a 7-Eleven. She's been in the country for only six months, but she's already learned that in America all small towns look alike, at least to a foreigner. She wonders if that's true of Poland too.

Jack turns onto a narrow street. The houses here are small and perfectly square. Chalk animals stand before a couple of them. In one yard she sees a pink flamingo. Christmas lights ring picture windows, tinsel hangs from trees glittering behind plate glass.

Jack parks at the edge of a driveway. They get out and walk across the yard toward the house. It's dark, but as they near the door, a porch light comes on.

Jack's father opens the door. He's a huge man, even larger than Jack. He has wavy gray hair and a red face. He's wearing a pair of glasses and a terry cloth bathrobe. In his right hand he holds what looks like a Luger. Porch light plays on the barrel.

He slips the pistol into the pocket of his robe and offers his hand to Jack. "Hey, son," he says. "How you been doing?"

Jack shakes his hand. "Fine," he says. "Good to see you."

Then Mr. Westbrook looks at her. "Good evening," he says, smiling broadly. "We sure are glad you come off down here to see us."

His accent is thicker than Jack's. For a moment she's afraid she won't be able to understand him. People from Mississippi have a love affair with vowels: they never seem willing to let them go.

"Hi," she says. "Was that a Luger you were holding?"

She can tell that he's impressed. "Sure is," he says. "I haggled with an old boy five years before he let me have it. Had to blackmail him even then. You interested in handguns?"

"Not really. But my father had one like that. He took it off a German officer during the Warsaw Uprising."

Mr. Westbrook laughs. "You won't have to worry about no Germans down here," he says. "We've got a lot of riff-raff, though. The town's seen three killings in the last year alone.

Folks just open up the door and get shot."

He leads them into the living room. Jack's mother and grandmother are waiting up. They're both small gray-haired women, indistinguishable, really, from one another. They both hug her. Then his grandmother—whose name is Annie—says she has to return to bed.

"I left my electric blanket on," she says, "and I hate to throw money away. If you ask me, electricity's a wasteful discovery."

Jack has told Malina that his grandmother still has every pair of shoes she's owned since the Great Depression. He says she and his grandfather, who died only last year, almost starved in 1930; she has never believed in her modest prosperity. It's a kind of behavior Malina thinks she understands. Every year as September approaches, her own grandmother begins to store food in preparation for a German offensive.

Thinking of her grandmother makes her edgy. It's two days before Christmas. This time last year, she and Adam were riding the express train to Olsztyn. This year, she knows, Adam plans to go alone. Two days from now, on Christmas Eve, she'll phone. She'll have to talk to her husband and her mother and her grandmother, wish them all a Merry Christmas, and do her best to evade questions about when she's coming home. Her exchange program takes an academic year, she will say. The academic year ends in May.

"Y'all must be hungry," Jack's mother, Darlene, is saying. "You want bacon and eggs or a sandwich?"

Jack pats his stomach. "Bacon and eggs," he says, "and I wouldn't mind some grits on the side."

Malina offers to help in the kitchen, but Darlene says she must be tired and orders her to rest. So she sits down on the couch in the wood-paneled den and listens to Jack and his father.

"Your grandmother," Mr. Westbrook says, "she's slipping fast, son." He glances at the door to the hallway, to make sure it's closed. "She's pinching pennies like never before, and she's convinced there's nothing ahead but disaster. She finally found a good deal on a monument for Henry, one of them his-and-hers markers, and they told her it'd be cheapest if she had as much of the engraving done right off as she could. So we go down there the other day to see it, and it's the damndest thing. On her side it says, Annie L. Pope. Born May 3, 1910. Died—and there's a blank spot—followed by a 1 and a 9. I looked at it and I said, 'Annie, what are you aiming to do if you live past the year 2000?' She gets this surprised look on her face, like she hadn't entertained that possibility. 'Well,' she says, 'I just can't afford to do that.'"

Jack and his father laugh, and she joins in. But at the same time, she thinks of the last talk she had with her grandmother, the week before she left for the U.S. "The next time you see me," her grandmother assured her, "I'll be stretched out under a slab on the hill above the lake. But I love that little lake. My husband and all my friends are buried there. There's no better place in the world to be dead."

She and Jack eat a huge greasy southern meal, during which Jack frequently praises his mother's cooking. Darlene beams as each forkful disappears into his mouth.

Tomorrow, Jack promises, Malina will prepare Hungarian stew for dinner; it's his favorite of all the dishes she's cooked for him during the last three months. He says you have to taste it to believe it.

She's shown to a bedroom across the hall from the one where Jack will sleep. Jack waits until they're alone in the hallway and embraces her.

Resting her cheek against the front of his shirt, she inhales his odor. The way he smells is one of many things she loves about him. He says it's the soap he uses, Irish Spring, combined with Brazilia, his cologne. The other night he proposed they put them together and market a new scent. They would call it Atlantic Crossing.

Now he says, "I'm so glad you came with me. I didn't think you'd agree to do it."

"I didn't think I would either," she says. "I just didn't want to miss the chance to spend Christmas with you."

"Maybe we'll spend other Christmases together."

"Maybe," she says.

He squeezes her tightly. "Good night," he says. "Get some sleep."

She wakes before dawn, feeling nauseated. Every item on her plate was soaked in Crisco. She already knows they'll expect her to eat the same type of food again at breakfast, so she makes up her mind to stay in bed late.

Jack works for a newspaper in Roanoke, Virginia. Malina met him at Virginia Tech, when he came to give a talk at the School of Communications. The title of his lecture was "The Development of Newspapers in the Deep South." She saw it advertised in the student paper and decided to attend. She wanted to learn as much about the country as she could, and she had a lot of empty hours to fill.

She can't remember much about the lecture. What she remembers is how hot the night was. It was the heat that led her to drink so much punch at the reception, and it was the punch that made her head foggy.

She found herself standing in a corner. She had stood in a lot of corners lately. A few American graduate students had invited her to parties, but when she got there she had a hard time talking with them. They never became more than a group of moving mouths, of gesturing hands and confident smiles. They kept breaking up into components—big white teeth, long pink nails.

That night at the reception she noticed that Jack was standing in a corner too. She'd seen a few people shake his hand right after the lecture, but from then on everybody ignored him. He kept refilling his cup, just like she did, and staring at the floor with a forced grin on his face. She'd begun to think Americans never felt uncomfortable; she was grateful to him for showing her that wasn't the case.

She drained her cup, walked over to him and told him she'd enjoyed his talk.

He laughed. "Doesn't look like anybody else did. I saw a

couple of people nodding off."

"I thought it was really informative."

"Hell, I hope it was," he said. "I'm not exactly academic. I spent most of last night digging through the *Encyclopedia of Southern Culture*, trying to come up with something to say. Problem was, I kept getting sidetracked. I read all the entries on blues and country music, and then I got off into the section on southern cooking. I'm from Mississippi," he said, "and I like to eat."

He wasn't fat, but he did have a belly. It strained at the fabric of his navy blue sweater.

She said, "Well, you sounded knowledgeable."

"If you don't mind my asking," he said, "where are you from?"

"Poland."

"I bet you like Szczypiorski."

None of her professors in the English department had heard of any Polish writers except Milosz and Herbert. She said, "How do you know about Szczypiorski?"

"I've always been interested in Holocaust novels," he said. "I read *The Beautiful Mrs. Seidenman* last year, and it knocked me out. I've got another one of his books at home, but I haven't read it yet."

She said, "I live in Warsaw, and I often see Szczypiorski drinking coffee and eating cheesecake at the Telimena Cafe." She loved to sit there herself, read a paper, and sip tea. She had not known how much she'd miss those daily pleasures.

"Next time you run across Szczypiorski," Jack said, "I wish you'd buy him a drink and tell him there's a guy in Virginia that thinks he's hot stuff."

She laughed. "Oh, I don't think I could do that. I don't know him personally."

He said she was probably right not to do it. In Boston a few years ago, he told her, he'd phoned his favorite American writer—it was someone she'd never even heard of—and asked if he could take him to dinner. The writer said yes. At the restaurant he was princely, but a few weeks later, when Jack called to tell him how much he liked his newest novel, he sounded delirious. "He kept saying, 'Sue me if you want to,'" Jack said, "and then he started crying. I finally hung up on him. That was my last contact with celebrity."

He looked around the room, then glanced at his watch. "I guess I've done my bit for American education. You want to go out and grab a drink?"

Evidently he had not noticed her ring. She wanted to go with him, wanted to sit in a bar with an American man and find out what that felt like, but she didn't know what it would mean if she did.

She said, "I've got an early class tomorrow. Maybe I should say no."

"Listen," he said, "do you have any idea what's happening right now, not more than six blocks from where we stand?"

"No."

"The Bluegrass Cardinals are in town."

"What are Bluegrass Cardinals?"

"Just a bunch of country boys with enough money to buy themselves some leisure suits and some nice guitars and banjos. In other words, a bluegrass band. A really good one."

"I've got a lot of Wordsworth to read," she said. "*The Prelude.*"

"Just imagine what your friends back in Warsaw'll say when they find out you had a chance to witness a whole performance by the Bluegrass Cardinals and passed it up for a prelude."

The bar was dark and smoky. On either side of the bandstand stood a massive totem pole. Most of the men in the room wore blue jeans and boots, plaid shirts, and cowboy hats. The women had long lashes, and their hair was stacked up high.

The band was good, the music fast and intricate. But the song lyrics were sentimental, and the lead singer sang them so seriously—eyes squeezed shut, a flutter in his voice—that she burst out laughing once or twice.

She and Jack sat in a booth at the rear of the room and drank one beer after another. They talked between songs and during the intermission. He asked her a string of questions—about her job, her apartment, Warsaw, Solidarity, Tyminski, Walesa, and Polish vodka. He said he'd read a lot of books set in Poland, and he'd love to see the country one day.

"And I've read Faulkner," she said. "I'd like to see Mississippi."

While they talked, she kept waiting for his face to break up. But despite all the beer some adhesive held him together.

I am looking at a person, she told herself. This man, this American, is an entity of substance, a thing of mass and feelings.

She wondered what he saw when he saw her. Did he think she had lived her whole life in a cage, that she'd spent entire days roaming the street, looking for something to eat? Would it stun him to discover that she owned a lot of books, a German car, one-half of a cottage on the Baltic coast, and that none of those possessions meant any more to her than they might have to him? Her heart pumped blood just like his did.

They kissed in the parking lot. He exuded a tropical odor.

"You know what?" she whispered. "I'm married. I should have told you."

"I saw your ring," he said. "I'm lonely. That's what I should have told you."

"You didn't need to. I figured it out."

Somebody drove by in a pickup truck and whistled.

He said, "I wish you'd come home with me."

"I want to," she said, "but my husband would never do this to me. If I go home with you, I'll feel horrible in the morning."

"I had hoped," he said, stroking her hair, "that we could put off the morning for a while."

She saw him almost daily but resisted moving in.

His house clung to a mountainside halfway between Blacksburg and Roanoke. When the wind blew, the branches of trees scraped the roof. At midnight a train rumbled by a few hundred feet below. He said it was the New River train, made famous in a bluegrass song.

"That's why I bought the house," he said.

The house had four bedrooms, two baths, a basement with a big wood stove. Every fifteen or twenty seconds, when you were taking a shower, the water would stop. It was something to do with a lack of pressure in the pump.

"I got the place cheap," he said, "because one day it'll slide down the mountain. By then I'll be gone."

"Gone where?"

"Mississippi."

"You want to move back?"

"Sure," he said. "It's home."

He was thirty-five and unmarried. His relationships with women, he said, tended to end badly. The only woman he'd ever lived with had left him because he refused to feed her goats.

He made a decent salary but spent most of it on records and books. He ate dinner at places like Bonanza and Wendy's. He never separated his clothes into colors when he washed them, so a given shirt might change hues three times in two weeks.

"It's the sartorial equivalent of recycling," he said.

He lay beside her for hours, kissing her hair, kissing her eyes, her fingers. He made her name her body parts in Polish.

They took long Sunday drives on the Blue Ridge Parkway. He'd vacationed in the mountains with his family. He pointed out a motel where they'd spent a night in 1963.

The mountains in autumn were burnt-orange and gold. Mornings were cold, but by noon the sun had burned the chill away. They lay on a blanket in a meadow near Galax, listening to old-time fiddlers. She loved a tune named "Soldier's Joy." It had come from some war, Jack was uncertain which.

He had never played chase among ruins, he did not know what treasures a bombed-out building offered. He had never worn unlined shoes to school through ankle-deep snow. His father had not disappeared in the fifties and returned with a limp and a lisp. Clicks and pops when he talked on the phone were not unnerving.

She had married her best friend. More than half her history was inseparable from his. He could finish singing any song she could start, he couldn't start a song she couldn't finish. She knew before he did when he wanted to leave the party. She could tell from the way he handled certain objects—ashtrays, coffee cups, keys—when something she had done was displeasing. If she came home late, he knew where she had been, which friend she had gone to visit. "How's Nina?" he would say. "Did she get her sink fixed?"

Too much of her life had been like that. She knew the other actors' moves and moods, she knew where all the props were. She knew when the lights would dim. She knew all her lines, and delivering them on cue was an easy thing to do. But every performance sapped a little more of her interest in the role.

This is it, she thought as she lay beside Jack in bed, the mountainside rumbling from the motion on the rails. *Real life is really beginning.*

She could swear she heard a banjo playing somewhere.

Annie, Jack's grandmother, is standing in the kitchen, looking at the small Polish cookbook that lies open on the countertop. Malina stuck the book in her bags as an afterthought the morning she left Warsaw.

Annie wrinkles her nose. "I can't make out none of this," she says. "I thought I'd be able to recognize a word here and there."

"I'll translate for you," Malina says. "The recipe calls for one-and-a-half pounds of pork with bones, three tablespoons flour, one medium onion, two-and-a-half tablespoons of fat for frying, five cups of sauerkraut, salt, ground paprika, one bay leaf, and red wine."

"Wine?"

Too late, Malina remembers that Annie is a staunch Baptist. According to Jack, she considers fermentation a diabolical process. "You just add a splash of the wine," she says.

"I've lived eighty-one years," Annie says, "without soaking up a single drop of alcohol."

It's starting to go badly, Malina thinks. She wishes Jack were here. He's out back with his father, looking at a new riding lawn mower. Why anyone would want to ride a lawn mower is beyond her. Darlene has gone Christmas shopping.

"A little wine," Malina says, "is good for the circulation."

Annie says, "You aim to keep circulating with Jackie?"

Malina doesn't know what to say. For obvious reasons, Jack hasn't told them that she's married.

"He wants everybody to think he likes living off up yonder in that house all alone, but that's really not true," Annie says. "When he was down here last Christmas, he told me 'Grandma, I'm lonesome.'"

Jack did not see his family last Christmas—he had to work—but the fact that Annie would lie to help secure his happiness makes Malina want to embrace her.

"I know that boy well," Annie says. "I think he wants to marry you. I bet he'd like to have babies."

She imagines her features melded with Jack's. She hears thin little voices crying *mamusia*, sees herself sitting in a rosewood rocker, nursing one baby after another. Adam has never wanted children. Whenever she brings up the subject, he has to take out the garbage or change the car oil.

She wipes her hands on the apron she's wearing. Her eyes have grown misty. She says, "I like Jack a lot, Annie. He'd make a wonderful father."

Annie puts her arm around her. Malina feels the frailness in her bones. "Don't you worry, Marlene," Annie says. "I'll eat your stew, alcohol and all."

While Malina prepares the meal, Annie hovers nearby, peppering her with questions about her family. Malina tells her that her father died five years ago, that her mother is healthy— she still works as a clerk in a bank—and her grandmother lives alone in a one-room apartment, in a city not far from the Lithuanian border.

"She was born in Warsaw," Malina says, chopping up the

onion on a cutting board, "but she moved away after the Second World War." She remembers the way her grandmother's voice crackles when she speaks about the basement she and Malina's mother lived in during the worst of the bombing. The only working stove was on the third floor; she had to risk her life to boil milk. "She left," Malina says, "because she didn't think they'd ever rebuild the city."

"That war messed Indianola up too," Annie says. "They tore down four nice houses so they could build an ugly armory. Spent a whole wad of money putting the thing up, and soon as they drove the last nail in, the darned war ended."

She shakes her head. Clearly the waste still disturbs her.

They eat dinner at a big table in the dining room. On a hutch nearby stand several pictures Malina first noticed last night. Jack at age six, dressed up like a cowboy, with fringe on his cuffs and shoulders. A graduation picture, in which he's wearing cap and gown, and a picture of him in his football uniform. He's the only child Darlene and Mr. Westbrook had, the only living creature they can cling to in old age.

Having only one person to hold on to, she thinks, must be a frightening prospect. She comes from a sizable family, has two sisters and a brother, a bunch of nieces and nephews. Three or four times a year they get together.

Forks flashing, knives clattering against their plates, the Westbrooks and Annie agree that Malina is a great cook. Darlene says, "What all's in this stew?"

Before Malina can reply, Annie says, "It's mostly stuff that you wouldn't think would fit together." She spears a piece of pork, as if to punctuate her statement. "A little of this and a little of that, but you mix it all up and it's nothing but nice."

Darlene says, "I want to get the recipe before y'all leave." She ducks her head girlishly and says, "Of course, I hope you'll come back."

Malina says, "I want to."

Want isn't *will*, and from the way Jack stares at his plate, she can tell he noted the verb choice.

Annie lifts her napkin, dabs her mouth and says, "Marlene,

honey, what part of Poland is Hungary in?"

She and Jack and Mr. Westbrook are in a pickup truck, on their way to the liquor store. The Luger is under the truckseat. It's Christmas Eve morning, and Mr. Westbrook has said that tonight, after his wife and mother-in-law are in bed, they'll all share a drink. He wants Malina to taste Wild Turkey.

Sometime this afternoon she'll have to phone Poland. By tonight, she thinks, she'll need a good drink. She's only spoken to Adam twice since she started seeing Jack. Both times he sounded worried, as if he feared that something was wrong but had no idea what. His letters betray the same concern. The other day he wrote *I can't wait until May. By the way, you haven't told us yet what day you'll be home. Doesn't an open ticket need to be revalidated? Don't forget to do that in advance.* He wrote those words at the desk in their bedroom, a small unfinished pine desk that they waited in line one cold morning to buy. They chose everything in their apartment together. All the items they own reflect consensus.

Mr. Westbrook drives them down the town's main street. Jack points out the Piggly Wiggly, the store where his mother buys her groceries; a Santa mannequin in the window turns from side to side. Silver bells dangle off the streetlights.

They make a left turn. Jack says, "There's the newspaper office." He jabs his finger at a building that looks like the shops you'd see in an American western: there's a big glass window with bold letters on it, an awning overhead. "The paper's called the *Enterprise-Tocsin*," Jack says. "It's good, but it could be better."

"I've been trying to talk Jack into buying it," Mr. Westbrook says.

Jack says, "With what?"

"There's plenty of folks here that'd still loan you money."

Jack turns to her and laughs. "How'd you like to be a reporter-copyeditor-typesetter-distribution manager-delivery-person?"

"You'll have to let me think about that."

The liquor store is out on the highway. She and Jack wait in the pickup while Mr. Westbrook goes in to buy the whiskey. It's warm in the pickup even without the heater on. The people on the streets aren't wearing coats, just sweaters or windbreakers. It's probably snowing now in Poland.

Jack takes her hand. Last night he came to her bedroom and sat beside her on the mattress. "That night I met you," he said, "I just wanted to take you to bed. I don't know what's happened. I ended up wanting more." He said he hoped bringing her here hadn't been a bad idea. She said it hadn't, she liked his family very much. But the truth is that Mississippi isn't Virginia, just as Hungary isn't Poland, and the house on the mountainside is too far away. For three months she's talked with almost no one but Jack. Now, suddenly, the rest of the world is back.

He says, "You look sad."

"I'm not sad," she says. "I just feel a little bit strange. This is the first Christmas I ever spent away from Poland."

"Are you thinking about your husband?"

"Do you want me to say I'm not?"

"It'd be odd if you weren't," he says. He looks out the window. Through the front of the store they can see his father. He's standing at the counter chatting with the man behind the register. Shelves filled with bottles line the walls. "You know, you've never really told me what Adam's like."

"He's a wonderful man," she says. She enumerates his fine points: he's honest, kind, hardworking, very bright. He's devoted to her. He would do almost anything she asked.

Jack tries a joke. "Sounds a lot like me."

"In some ways," she says, "I guess he is. Probably the biggest difference in Adam and you is that you've made me fall in love and he was never able to."

Mr. Westbrook comes out of the store with a brown bag under his arm. He gets in the truck and hands her the whiskey. "This stuff'll make you see double," he says. "But since I'm starting to lose my eyesight, I figure I can stand a little extra ocular power." For the first time she notices just how thick his lenses are.

On the way home, he stops the truck near a green board fence. Through the spaces between the boards, she sees old cars piled up on one another. On a light pole, about twenty feet above the ground, rests a rusty red Volkswagen Beetle. A legend on one door says A & H USED PARTS.

Mr. Westbrook says, "That's nothing but the shell of the car on the pole. Every year or two they have to put another one up there. It rains a lot here, and old cars on poles rust out pretty quick."

He says the reason he stopped here has nothing to do with junked cars. "Back in the forties," he says, "this junkyard was used as a POW camp."

Jack says, "I didn't know that."

The camp never had more than ten or fifteen prisoners, Mr. Westbrook tells Malina. The camp commander hired them out to local farmers. He didn't worry much about escape, because there was nowhere the prisoners could go except Greenwood or Leland.

Mr. Westbrook says his father worked the POWs in his cotton fields. "The prisoners were German," he says, "and by and large a sullen bunch. One or two of 'em could speak a little English, but not much. Daddy used 'em to chop cotton along about July.

"There was one old boy that kept claiming he wasn't one of them. He swore up and down he was Polish. Said they took him prisoner and made him serve in the Wehrmacht. You ever hear of anything like that happening?"

"There were many instances of it," she says. "Mostly in the south and southwestern parts of Poland. There were a lot of people of German origin in those areas who spoke Polish and considered themselves Polish, but the Germans didn't agree."

"Daddy always thought the boy was lying," Mr. Westbrook says, "but I couldn't help but believe he was telling the truth. The others didn't seem to have much use for him, and I figured that was a good sign." He shakes his head. "I can still remember the name of the place he said he was from—a town called Gliwice," he says, getting the pronunciation almost right. "Just saying that word made his voice break."

She can see him: a big Silesian boy in his early twenties with hair the color of straw. For all he knows, everyone he loves is dead. He leans on his hoe in sweltering heat, in a field six thousand miles from home. Mosquitoes buzz near his face. Slowly he pronounces the name of a place. The sound of the word is all he has left.

She feels as if a sock has been stuffed into her throat. "What happened to him?" she says.

"I don't know—they sent 'em someplace else," Mr. Westbrook says. He releases the clutch and pulls into the road. "But I've always liked to think that somehow he made it back to Gliwice."

After lunch she and Annie and Jack visit the cemetery. Annie intends to lay a plastic wreath on the grave of her husband. She has chosen plastic, Jack says, because it can be used again next year. She's a little bit worried that it might be stolen.

The cemetery looks just like the cemetery in Blacksburg. Most of the markers are small, and there are no slabs over the graves like there would be in Poland. The street runs close to the spot where Jack's grandfather lies.

They park the car and walk across the brown grass. Jack's grandfather's marker has two granite pillars. She notices the dates by Annie's name.

Annie leans over and places the wreath at the head of the grave. "He was an awfully good man," she tells Malina. "I'll be proud to lay next to him through eternity."

Jack puts one arm around Annie and another around Malina. "I wish Grandpa could have met you," he tells Malina.

"He sure would have liked her," says Annie.

For a moment they stand there, Malina bound to Annie by Jack. He has brought them together. A woman born in Mississippi in 1910 and a woman half a century younger from the Mazurian Lakes. She marvels at his power to pull her— even as, with one gentle motion, she begins to draw away.

She's standing at a small table in the den. Jack and his parents and Annie are lined up on the living room couch. The three of them talk quietly, the lights from the tree throwing various shades upon their faces. She can see them in there, she can hear their voices, but the sounds they're making refuse to form words.

She's holding the receiver close to her ear. The last five times she dialed, the call failed to go through.

She hears the long series of beeps that signal a successful attempt. The phone in her mother's apartment begins to ring.

Her grandmother, legs swollen and breath coming short, puts her hand to her mouth. Adam's fingertips whiten on the arms of his chair. Her mother is already there, lifting the receiver.

There's a carol on the stereo. *Lulajze Jezuniu*, "Hush, Little Jesus." It's a badly scarred record, one she listened to as a child. She hears the old song clearly, even here in this new world.

"Malina," her mother says, "we've been waiting."

"I know," she says. "I have too."

"How are you?"

"I'm fine. How's Grandmother?"

Her mother hands her grandmother the phone. She hears the labored breathing. "Malina," her grandmother says, "I'm alive again at Christmas."

It's as if she's opened a gift box and found another year inside.

"I know you are," says Malina, "and I'm grateful."

"When will you come home? No, wait, Adam wants to hear you say it. He's having silly ideas."

When he comes on the phone, he sounds tentative. "Malina?"

She remembers an attic apartment in West Berlin. It belonged to a friend, who let them live there one summer when they were working illegally. At night they lay awake listening to a street singer who looked for all the world like Herzog's Strosek. He played the accordion, and they always wanted to give him money, but the marks were what they had come for. She worked all day in an *eis bistro*; Adam made rolls in a bakery. They earned enough to buy a Volkswagen in decent condition, and they drove it all over Germany and into Belgium before it was time to go home.

Berlin is no longer divided, but she knows she is, knows that in some sense she always will be. There's a corner of herself she will have to wall off. For the most part she'll probably succeed. But someday, she thinks, some ordinary day, when she's loitering on a street in the Old Town, looking at French fashions through a shop window or admiring leather goods at a sidewalk bazaar, a sound will stop her heart. Wafting toward her on the breezes of a Warsaw autumn, as light as the fingers that pluck it, the tinkling music of a five-string banjo played in the Old Town Square.

Black Angus

"This is the beginning of my last day as a white man," Dad said. "Starting tomorrow I'm a glorified nigger."

It was a Saturday morning in February of 1962. We were sitting at the breakfast table, surrounded by Clorox boxes filled with pots and pans and cans of hominy and pork and beans. Momma had packed up the bulk of the kitchen stuff last night. Most of it we wouldn't be needing for a while, not till we got our own place again. When that would be I didn't know. Dad was going to drive a tractor for Grandpa this year, and we'd be living in the house with him and Grandma.

I didn't say so that morning, but it seemed to me that a glorified nigger, while not the best thing to be, was not the worst thing either. There were two black families on our place. I didn't know if they were glorified or not, but I did know that when we left, they'd be staying put. I'd heard Dad say they'd made a deal with the new man—the man who'd be moving into our house next week, whose kids would be sleeping in my room and hurling baseballs at the backstop Dad had built for me.

The morning was a sunny one but cold. I was wearing the Ole Miss sweatshirt Grandma had given me at Christmas and a thick jacket too, but the chill cut through them.

There had been a hard frost during the night; walking back and forth across the yard between the road and the tractor shed, we felt the brown grass crunch under our feet. I spent several hours out there helping Dad get everything ready. I held trailer tongues up and let him back the tractors up to them, I stuck the hitch pins into the drawbars. I dragged empty cotton sacks over to one of the trailers and threw them over the sides, then I lugged over a bunch of odds and ends—an empty tool box, Dad's tackle box, the fishing poles we never used—and pitched them inside too.

I squatted nearby and held Dad's tools as he unhooked our Lerio pump and capped off the water pipes. "If that son of a bitch Stacy wants water in the house," he said, teeth clenched, while he tightened a Stillson wrench, "he can go out and buy his own goddamn pump. I paid a hundred dollars for mine."

Stacy was the new man. Mr. Parker, who owned the eighty acres we'd been renting for almost eight years, had told Dad Stacy was offering him twenty dollars an acre for a three-year lease. He said if Dad could meet that offer we could stay. But Dad said no. Now the day had come for us to leave.

The house was the only one I'd ever lived in. I knew which floorboards would pop up if I stomped them just right, how to swing onto the tin roof from the cypress tree out back, how to climb off again before anybody caught me. I'd made several friends at Moorhead Elementary. The school in Indianola was a lot bigger, and I didn't know a soul there. For the last few weeks, ever since Momma had told me we'd be moving, I'd dreaded this morning. I feared it like I used to fear the snakes that sometimes chased me in my dreams. Sooner or later it would overtake me, just as the snakes had, but this time waking up wouldn't solve a thing.

Dad backed the truck up to the pumphouse. Grunting and straining, we heaved the Lerio up onto the tailgate, then Dad climbed in and tugged it toward the cab. We pulled down the mesh wire that fenced our garden—turnips and collards were still growing there—and laid it in the back of the truck behind the pump.

We went back inside to let Momma know we were leaving with the first load. She was in the kitchen, sweeping the floor.

"What you doing that for?" Dad said.

She didn't look up, just kept on sweeping. "Best I can remember," she said, "the floor was clean when we moved in. I don't like to leave things worse off than I found them."

"The place has left us a lot worse off than we were when we moved in."

"It's not the place that did that. It's the times."

"Suit yourself," Dad said. "Personally, I'd just as soon the roof fell in on Stacy the first night he sleeps here."

I saw eye to eye with Momma more often than not; right now, though, I agreed with Dad. I didn't know who Stacy was or where he'd come from, but I'd discovered it was possible to hate somebody without ever seeing his face. All you had to do was reduce him in your mind to the negative effect his actions had on you. Because I could do that, I hated Stacy almost as much as I hated Mr. Parker, whose face I knew perfectly well.

Apparently I was destined to see Mr. Parker's face that morning. When we got in the truck, Dad said, "We need to stop by old man Parker's. He asked me to bring you by this morning. Said him and Mrs. Parker wanted to see you."

"What for?"

He cranked the truck. "Who the hell knows? How could somebody like me know what folks like them think?" He pulled into the road and headed for town.

The Parkers lived on First Street, in a big white Victorian-style house. I'd been inside that house many times—I often went with Momma when she carried the rent checks by. Whenever we went there, Mrs. Parker offered Momma coffee and me lemonade, and she usually put some cookies on a plate, and I ate those. She was a small, white-haired lady who always wore neat dresses and kept her hair pulled back into a bun. Now, I'd heard, she was sick. The last two times Momma and I had gone by, Mr. Parker had met us at the front door and accepted the checks himself. He never invited us in.

Dad parked on the street in front of their house. Their car was in the driveway. The car was a big pink one, with extra-wide tires and a long ventilated hood. Mr. Parker liked to drive that car fast. On Saturdays, when Momma took me into town to get a milk shake at Johnson's Drug Store, we'd sometimes hear a loud roar, and then, a few seconds later, we'd see the pink car blazing down the street, headed for the highway and Greenwood or Indianola.

"That's a Stutz Bearcat," Dad said. "You know what it cost?"

"A lot?"

"More than your momma and me'll make in any ten years." He shook his head. "Look at the pink son of a bitch. It's the envy of every pimp in the Delta."

We rang the doorbell, but no one answered.

"Maybe they're not here," I said.

"They're here. They're just not in any hurry. Our time's not precious to them."

Finally Mr. Parker opened the door. He was a big red-faced man whose cheeks looked flabby. He wore a shiny bathrobe that was about the same shade of pink as his car. The legs of his pajamas were striped like canes of peppermint candy.

"Come on in, Paul," he said. "Mrs. Parker and me have just finished breakfast."

He stood aside. I started in, but Dad grabbed my arm. "Wipe your feet," he said. I did, even though I knew there was nothing on my shoes.

Mr. Parker led us into the living room. There was a couch there and three or four armchairs and a coffee table. Built-in bookshelves lined one whole wall, the shelves filled with tall, thick, leather-bound books that Mrs. Parker used to invite me to look at. Her tea service stood on a sideboard in one corner, and in another was her daughter's piano. The daughter, who had died four or five years ago, had never gotten married. She'd lived her whole life in this house with her mother and father. I remembered her fairly well. She'd been a tall girl, big-boned like Mr. Parker. She used to play for the choir at the Methodist Church.

"Won't y'all make yourselves at home?" Mr. Parker said. "Let me hang your coats up."

We gave him our jackets, then I walked over to the couch and sat down. Before choosing one of the armchairs, Dad swiped at the seat of his pants with one hand, like he thought there was something there that would damage any surface it contacted.

"Would y'all like some coffee?" Mr. Parker said. "Or maybe a little nip of some good whiskey for you, Paul?"

"No, thank you. We need to hit the road. We got a bunch of stuff to move before dark."

"I'll go see if I can hurry Mrs. Parker. She's upstairs. She's a little bit slow these days because of her illness."

He climbed the stairs, and when I was sure he wouldn't hear me, I leaned toward Dad and whispered, "What's wrong with Mrs. Parker?"

Dad was sitting there rigid, his big hands lying on his thighs. He reminded me of a picture my teacher had taped up on the wall at school. It was a photo of the Lincoln Memorial. "My guess is she's got what their girl had," he said.

"What was that?"

"Cancer. Lots of times parents and kids get the same diseases."

They came back down together, Mrs. Parker leaning on Mr. Parker's arm. You could tell from looking at her that she was awfully sick. She had lost weight in the months since I'd seen her; the skin on her cheeks looked paper thin. It was a funny color too, not exactly blue but not too far from it. Her hair was still neat, though; she still wore it pulled back into that bun.

Dad stood up. "Hi, Mrs. Parker," he said.

"Hello, Mr. Lucas. Good morning, Terry."

She reached over the coffee table and offered me her hand. I didn't want to touch it but I did, and then I knew I'd been right not to want to. It was ice cold. It occurred to me that before very long, she'd probably be dead.

She sat down in one of the armchairs. "Did you offer them something to drink?" she said. "Terry likes lemonade, I believe."

Dad said, "Mrs. Parker, we're in a little bit of a hurry."

"You're moving over to Indianola, is that right?"

"Yes, ma'am."

"To live with Mrs. Lucas's parents?"

"That's right."

"I was born over there," Mrs. Parker said. "On the Fairview Plantation. There's some excellent land around the Sunflower River."

"Yes, ma'am," Dad said. "I wouldn't mind owning a little chunk of it."

"A lot of people wouldn't mind owning a chunk of it," Mr. Parker said. "Me, for instance."

He'd perched on the arm of Mrs. Parker's chair. His hand lay on her shoulder. Every few seconds he'd pat her softly, like Momma used to pat me when I was sick with a fever. It surprised me to see him do that. I associated him with speed and noise, not gentle, quiet gestures.

"It's ownership, I suppose, that I asked you to come by and talk about," Mrs. Parker told Dad. "Accepting the higher rent offer was purely a business decision. It doesn't reflect our attitude toward you and your family in any way. You've been the finest tenants Mr. Parker and I have ever had. We want you to know that."

"Absolutely," Mr. Parker said. "You've been good as gold, Paul."

"I'm especially grateful," Mrs. Parker went on, "that I got a chance to know Terry here. I think he's an unusual young man. I'm sure you know that Mrs. Lucas used to bring him by with her when she delivered the rent checks. I noticed that he loves to look at books and hold them in his hands, and he was always interested in the piano too. He reminds me of our daughter in that way. You don't see too many young people who love books and music anymore—at least not good books or good music."

My face was probably red—I know it was hot. I felt a little like I had a year or two ago when I was taking a bath and the preacher came by. I sat there in the tub for almost an hour, the water turning ice cold, while in the next room he talked to Momma and Dad about my soul. He said he thought I was ready to join the church because I acted restless during the hymn of invitation. But if I acted restless, it was only because

I wanted to get out, to go home and turn on the TV set.

I had handled Mrs. Parker's books, I believed, not because I liked the feel of such books in my hands, but because I knew she liked to see me do it, and I wanted to make sure to please her so she'd keep offering me the lemonade and cookies. And now I wished I hadn't done that; I'd pleased her enough to keep the cookies coming, but I hadn't pleased her enough to stop her and her husband from raising the rent on Dad and taking away our house. She'd never know what losing a house felt like.

"Terry's the kind of boy who ought one day to attend college," Mrs. Parker said. "I notice he's wearing an Ole Miss sweatshirt. That's a perfectly good school. I attended the W— MSCW, it's actually called. Have you ever heard of that, Terry?"

"No, ma'am."

"It stands for Mississippi State College for Women. It's over in Columbus, near the Alabama line. I got a fine education there. The problem is, a college education is expensive. Even if you go to a state-supported university—Ole Miss, for instance—there's a lot of cost associated with it. Tuition, room and board, books. All those things cost money."

I remembered a story my mother had once told me about the time somebody tried to buy her. She said a man and a woman had driven up to her parents' house one day when she was four years old. She and my grandparents were living east of Rolling Fork then, and Grandpa was working WPA, helping build the Yazoo County Courthouse. This was in the middle of the Great Depression.

The couple drove a shiny black car that had silver hubcaps and a little silver ornament on the hood. The man got out and looked across the yard at the porch, trying to see if there was any way to get to the front steps from where he stood without muddying his shoes. He finally decided there wasn't and began to pick his way through the puddles and the dog and chicken droppings.

Momma said the woman never did get out of the car. The

man came in by himself, and while Momma sat on the floor playing with a rag doll, he told Grandpa that he and his wife could give Momma things she'd never have otherwise, that they lived in a big house in Jackson and owned three grocery stores and wanted a little girl more than anything in the world. He said they could take Momma to Europe and send her to college and buy her a place of her own when she grew up. When the man finished, Grandpa looked at Grandma. She didn't say a word to him, but something must have passed between them. He got up and walked over to the front door and opened it and motioned at the man. "I guess we all want what we don't have," Grandpa said, "but at least right now you've got your life, though that could change any minute." The man and his wife drove away fast, the black car slinging mud.

I wanted to warn Dad, to let him know that this woman who was already half-dead was about to offer to take me, to let me live here in the house with her and Mr. Parker and ride in their pink car all the way to Ole Miss. I didn't think for one second that Dad would agree, but I was afraid the proposal would make him so mad he'd jump out of his chair and hurt Mr. Parker. And hurting Mr. Parker would cause trouble, I believed, more trouble than we'd ever known in our lives.

"We've got a small herd of Black Angus," Mrs. Parker said. "We'd like to give them to Terry."

"Fine beef cattle," Mr. Parker said. He grinned at me. "Good as gold."

"By saying we'd like to give them to him," Mrs. Parker said, "I don't mean, Mr. Lucas, that you'd be responsible for feeding and maintaining the herd. We'd send them to the auction in Winona and the proceeds would go into a savings account in Terry's name. The money could be withdrawn when he turns eighteen and gets ready to attend college. It won't cover everything, of course, but at least it would be a start."

Dad did not jump out of his chair and hit Mr. Parker. He would not have jumped out of his chair, I can see now, and hit Mr. Parker, or threatened to, even if Mrs. Parker had made the same kind of offer the man had made my grandpa in the thirties. Before I was born, Dad had worked at eight or nine different jobs, farmed two or three different patches of land, had to move four or five times—all before he turned thirty. He was used to seeing things go wrong, but he knew there was no point expressing anger or displeasure to anybody except the two people at home. Nobody else cared much one way or the other what his mood was.

Whatever he felt about being offered the herd of Black Angus he kept to himself. He said, "That's real kind of you, Mrs. Parker. I guess it's up to Terry to say."

"Terry," Mrs. Parker said, "would you like to have the cattle?"

I did go to college, but not to Ole Miss. I attended a university on the West Coast in the mid-seventies, and for four years I sat through a series of courses in which the forces that operated on my father and me that day, and on Mr. and Mrs. Parker, too, were scrutinized and analyzed. I learned various theories that efficiently explained my behavior on that morning; at one time or another I accepted most of them, though I reject them all now, mostly because they're efficient.

I know a professional photographer who once showed me two photos he had taken in an African village, one of those places where everyone is starving. In the first photo there's a child with hungry eyes, sores on his face, a belly so distended it looks like there's a basketball inside it. The child gazes straight into the camera; it's almost as if he's soliciting aid— and the picture actually was used a few years ago in newspaper ads sponsored by a British relief agency.

The second picture would not be useful in such ads. There are two children in it, and they look a lot like the child in the first photo. They wear nothing but rags; their stomachs are swollen; their eyes burn with hunger. One of them is sitting on the ground in the mud, his thin arms covering his head, while the other one beats him on the shoulders with a limb. You wonder that somebody so weak and hungry could pick up a limb, much less swing it with such force.

You suppose they may be fighting over a piece of stale bread or some other possession you would find worthless—maybe an old shoe with a hole in the sole, which some relief worker from the U.S. or Western Europe left behind. In fact, according to my friend who took the picture, the child swinging the branch is attacking the other child for saying that he can't carry a tune, that he's got an ugly voice and ought to give up singing.

My behavior toward Mrs. Parker that morning makes the same kind of sense to me now as the second photo has made ever since I learned the reason for the beating.

When she asked me if I wanted the herd of Black Angus, I looked right at her, at that face that was slowly turning blue as the skin died on her cheeks, and I told her, "No, ma'am."

"I see," she said. "And would you mind telling me why?"

I took my time giving her an answer. And when I did give it, it probably surprised me more than it did her.

"I don't want to go to college," I said. "I don't want to learn anything more than I know right now."

Dad cranked the pickup, but he didn't pull away from the curb. He pointed at the Stutz Bearcat and said, "You know what Old Man Parker did one time in that car?"

He sounded very calm, almost happy. And almost happy was as close to happy as he ever came in his life.

"No sir," I said. "What?"

"He went off down to Florida in it to go deep-sea fishing with his brother that lives in Miami. And while he was down there, the National Weather Service issued a hurricane warning. This was seven or eight years ago, before their girl died, and I can't remember which hurricane was coming, but it was a bad one. So Old Man Parker sat around his brother's house there, drinking whiskey and waiting till the waves started getting tall, and then he got in that big car over yonder, and he flat outran that hurricane. He was sitting in Birmingham eating supper before the damned storm made it to the Alabama line."

He pulled into the street. "You remember one thing," he said. "There's nothing you can't outrun in a car like that one."

Like he'd said, the same diseases often afflict parents and their children, and for a long time the disease that afflicted him afflicted me. It was a willingness to believe in the simple answer, the truth that strikes you hard like a moving mass of metal.

On the road to Indianola I closed my eyes and envisioned Mr. Parker at the wheel of the pink Stutz Bearcat. I saw him driving fast on wet asphalt, pulling into the left lane every now and then to pass slower cars or occasionally a pickup truck filled with the belongings of an entire family—a bed, a kitchen table, two or three old chairs with the stuffing poking out. From time to time, the drivers of those cars and trucks glanced backwards, toward Miami, where trees and light poles were going down, where the air was filled with sand and shingles and shards of window glass. Black waves crashed over the seawall, flooding people's houses; then the wind blew the houses away.

But Mr. Parker kept his eyes on the road ahead, on the white line that led to Alabama. Unlike the other drivers, he never looked over his shoulder. He never worried about the trouble that lay behind him.

$\mathcal{A}$ Life of Ease

Saturday morning, when Pat Dodd pushed her basket up to the check-out stand, she noticed that the woman in front of her had two little boys, and they were both sporting University of Alabama T-shirts. Only the Aikmans would be wearing Crimson Tide apparel in Indianola, Mississippi.

Pat hadn't met the new preacher yet. She'd been visiting her mother the day he came for his interview. But her husband, Nick, who'd played the major role in Aikman's hiring, had assured her he was a firebrand from way back. A big blond guy who'd played football in college, he could boom and he could whisper. If he took a notion to pound the pulpit, you felt like it just might splinter. Nick said he'd be a great ministerial presence.

Pat studied Sally Aikman. She was small and dark haired. She intently watched the register, checking the price of each item as the cashier rang it up. Her fingertips tapped a nervous rhythm on the countertop.

Just as Pat was about to introduce herself, the older of the two boys grabbed a bag of miniature Milky Ways from a bin and shoved them at his mother. "Momma, let's get these. Please."

Sally Aikman pulled them out of his hand and tossed them back into the bin. "You don't need them," she said, "and anyway, they cost too much. Your daddy's not making much money."

Pat pulled her cart away from the stand as if she'd forgotten something. She didn't want to embarrass Sally Aikman, and she didn't want to embarrass herself. Her husband chaired the board of deacons, and the board set Aikman's salary.

She sat on the edge of the bed in her slip, watching Nick rub Johnson's Baby Powder into his scalp. He always powdered his head on Sunday morning. The overhead lights at Beaverdam Baptist were harsh and bright, and he was sensitive about being bald. He'd lost most of his hair before he turned thirty.

He glanced over his shoulder at her. "Seeing you like that," he said, "makes me have ungodlike thoughts."

"What's ungodlike about them?"

"They're a little too earthy."

"What's wrong with the earth?"

"Earth's dirt."

"And God's air?"

"God's light."

"If God's light," she said, "He shines on dirt too."

The back of his neck had turned a telltale pink. In a second, if she didn't put her clothes on, he'd be out of his suit pants. She stood and pulled on her dress.

She and Nick and the kids always sat on the left side of the church, in the third pew from the front. No matter how late they arrived, that pew was always empty. No one ever joined them except at Christmas or Easter, when the sanctuary filled up.

The organist was playing "Sweet Hour of Prayer" when Joe Aikman stepped through the door near the baptistry. He took a seat on the podium next to the song leader. He seemed like anything in the world but a firebrand. His hair had a boyish wave in it, and he didn't look a day beyond twenty. Nick had said he was thirty-one.

After the opening hymn, Aikman filled the pulpit. He gazed out at the congregation and smiled. "I wanted this church bad," he said. "I felt like it was the only place I belonged.

"I know a lot of you get up in the morning and think about your problems, and you feel like if it wasn't for your faith, you'd waft away on the wind. You feel little, feel light, feel like to most folks you don't matter.

"And the truth is that to most folks you don't. Brothers and sisters, I'm here to tell you that to the politicians in Washington, you don't matter. Your votes matter, but not too much, because it's a little bit embarrassing to get them. To the folks that run the corporations, you don't matter. Your money matters, but not too much because most of you don't have enough of it.

"We say this country's a democracy, but it's not. No country is. Nobody sitting here thinks his voice, if he raised it as loud as he could, would be heard above the voices of the very rich and mighty.

"In fact, there's only one democracy, and the paradox is it's ruled by a monarch. But that monarch said *When the poor and the needy seek water and there is none, and their tongue faileth for thirst, I the Lord will hear them, I the God of Israel will not forsake them. I will open rivers in high places, and mountains in the midst of the valleys. I will make the wilderness a pool of water, and the dry land springs of water.*

"Either you know this is so or you don't. Once upon a time I didn't. Once upon a time you all didn't either. But now by the grace of God we do. Thank you all, from the bottom of my heart, for calling me to be your minister."

After the service, on the way home, Nick said, "We may have got more than we bargained for. Sounds to me like the preacher we've hired is some sort of revolutionary." He made a sour face. "The very rich and mighty. If two or three of us didn't have a little money in the bank, he wouldn't draw his salary."

Pat stared out her window at a cotton field. She thought it was one of theirs. Nick owned more than three thousand acres and kept expanding every year.

She said, "Well, we could all stand a little shaking up. At least I know I could."

Joe Aikman sat at the table watching as Sally moved silently around the kitchen, washing dishes, checking on the bacon she was frying. There was something quiet but furious in her motion, some pent-up wrath that he wished would erupt.

He said, "I didn't mean to sleep so late. Why didn't you wake me?"

"Why would I?"

He let the question go unanswered. "Did the boys get off okay?"

"Do you see them here?"

He sat still for a minute, then he rose and walked over to the pantry. He opened the door and looked inside. He got down on his knees and peered under the bottom shelf. "Just some industrial-sized hominy and pork-and-beans down here." He closed the pantry door and walked over to the counter. He stooped and started opening the cabinets one by one. He pulled out pots, removed their lids. She stood still now, watching him.

He closed the last door. "Nope," he said, grinning at her, "I can't find the boys anywhere. Guess that means they did get off okay."

She turned away, went back to the stove.

It was like that lately whenever they were alone. If he woke in time to eat breakfast with the boys, she'd be polite to him until the school bus had come and gone. Then she'd turn the ice on. He usually tried to get to the church as fast as he could, and he rarely returned until three-thirty, when the boys would be home.

His marriage had never been perfect, but at various times it had been okay. He'd met Sally in college at a postgame party. She'd slept with him on their fourth date, and sometime between then and the day they got married—five months later—he'd made her pregnant. She quit school to have the baby. He fooled around and failed to graduate.

She hadn't come from a wealthy family. But she'd never been as poor as she was with him after the baby was born. Jack had asthma, and the steroid treatments the doctor ordered left them broke. She got pregnant again, too.

He was working at Safeway when Tony was born. For a while that year he stole a lot of what they ate. As chief of the night crew, he locked the store each morning at four o'clock, and he always left with a grocery sack filled up. He never really felt like he was stealing. He was just taking what an easier lot in life would have left him able to buy.

One day, in the midst of an argument over money, he made the mistake of telling her how he'd come by their groceries. She cried for hours, and no number of sweet nothings softly whispered could convince her they hadn't dead-ended.

He went out that night and drank half a week's pay. The next morning, hungover and sick to his stomach, he found himself sitting in the back pew of a Baptist church, capable of nothing but surrender. If a gun had been available, he would have turned it on himself, and if someone had offered him drugs he would have taken them. Instead he mainlined faith. To his surprise it had never worn off.

When he decided to enter the seminary, Sally took a night job at a 7-Eleven to help pay the bills. They were living in Bessemer at the time, and her parents were close by; they finally had a chance to get away from the kids on occasion, go out for a movie or a pizza, and those evenings alone made things a lot better.

Then he got the offer to preach at First Baptist in Biloxi, where the parsonage was a big two-story house overhung with Spanish moss and the salary was thirty thousand dollars. Instead of taking that offer, he told her he believed God wanted them up here at a small rural church in the Delta, just about the poorest place in the United States.

She had said, "You think you'll go back up there and save your dad?"

"My dad's dead," he said. "And I can't save anybody. All I am is a messenger, but I believe the package I'm carrying's addressed to folks up there."

Even now he believed his decision had been the right one. But he'd been paying for it since the day he made it, and it seemed like the bill kept mounting.

He ate his breakfast, showered and dressed and drove to

the church. He spent an hour in his study, drafting his Sunday morning sermon. He was just about to take a break when he heard a car pull into the gravel lot.

He peered through a slit in the blinds: it was Nick Dodd's wife. She tipped her sunglasses up as she got out of her car. She wore a pair of tight Levi's and a white cotton blouse cinched at the waist by a black cord.

Each of the past three Sundays, as he preached his sermon, he'd had to remind himself of a lecture he'd attended at the seminary. The title of the lecture was "Comportment in the Pulpit." The minister who delivered it told an anecdote about a friend of his, a man who'd stared a little too long at an attractive member of his congregation. One night she came to his house and refused to leave until he agreed to step outside with her. While his wife gazed out the window, the woman embraced him and told him she loved him, and when he tried to pull away, she seized his forearm and bit a plug out of it.

"That was the end of his effectiveness as a minister," the lecturer said. "He knew he hadn't done anything but stare and the Lord knew it too. But everybody else had their doubts."

Aikman found it hard not to stare at Pat Dodd. She was a beautiful woman: tall and nicely tanned, with trim hips and full breasts. But what really attracted him was the expression in her eyes. She seemed to look at the whole world, him included, with a complete lack of interest, like she'd seen everything twice and been bored both times.

He opened the door. She said, "Hi, Brother Joe. I was driving by, and I thought I'd stop."

"Come on in."

She walked over to one of the armchairs in front of his desk and sat down. She crossed her legs. "Do you mind," she said, "if I smoke?"

He pulled out a pack of Camels. "Do you mind if I join you?"

"I didn't know you were a smoker."

"It's not something I'm eager to advertise. I usually have a cigarette when I take a break from writing my sermons. I feel bad about it, but it helps me relax."

He sat down in his swivel chair. He withdrew a lighter from his pocket, reached across the desk, and thumbed the flint. When she leaned over to light her cigarette, he could see down the front of her blouse. She wasn't wearing a bra.

She sucked smoke into her lungs and puffed it out. "Your sermons are the best I've ever heard," she said. "I wanted to tell you that."

"Thank you. I work hard on them, but finding the right words is a matter of luck. Or grace."

"They seem crafted for this particular church," she said. "Most of the people here are small farmers, and their lives are filled with trouble."

When he was twelve and living down in the southern part of the Delta, Aikman had watched his father lose a lot of his farm equipment to the Bank of Lexington. The next year, barring a miracle, he probably would have lost the farm itself.

Evidently his father had not believed in miracles. One day, when Aikman was sitting in third-period English, the principal came and got him and walked him to the office, where he found his mother leaning against the wall, a handkerchief pressed to her face.

"Joe," the principal said, "something pretty awful's happened."

Later, after his mother remarried and they moved to Alabama and he could think about Lexington, Mississippi, and his father without crying, Aikman constructed a list of all the people who might have done something for his dad. The one thing they all had in common was unlimited access to large sums of money.

Now, as he looked at the Rolex on Pat Dodd's wrist and thought about the new Volvo wagon that stood parked outside, he couldn't help but wonder what she knew about lives filled with trouble. It looked to him like she led a life of ease.

She went on about his sermons. They were so articulate, she said, yet so simply written. She told him that the previous minister, who'd been seventy when he retired, had always tried to sound professorial.

"He knew a lot of multisyllabic words," she said, "but he didn't know what most of them meant. He was big on *mellifluous,* which he thought was a noun."

Aikman laughed. *"Mellifluous,"* he said, "is a word I haven't had much call for."

"Nor does anybody else around here."

She had smoked her cigarette down to a nub. "Well," she said, glancing at the Rolex, "I guess I better get home."

She didn't stop by again for a couple of weeks. But after that, her visits became a lot more frequent. She always pulled a cigarette out and let him light it for her, and he usually smoked one too. She'd sit there talking for an hour or more.

Sometimes she talked about his sermons, sometimes she talked about upcoming church functions. Sometimes she talked about the news that had graced the morning paper's front page. But no matter what she talked about, she talked as if he was the only person in the world who would listen.

Every time she left his office, he would sit at his desk, inhaling the odor of her perfume. It did not smell much like the kind Sally wore.

That fall he settled into his ministerial routine. Sunday services morning and night, Brotherhood on Wednesday night, Saturday morning prayer breakfasts. He preached several funerals and married one teenaged couple that he doubted would stay together more than a year.

The summer had been unusually dry and hot, the fall cold and rainy. Cotton that hadn't burned in June mildewed in October and sold below grade. There was a strike on at Southern Prime, the big catfish processing plant in town. Several of the smaller catfish farmers in his congregation couldn't get any fish processed because the plant was backed up.

There was plenty of pain to go around, and Aikman spent a lot of time at peoples' homes, praying for some sunshine to fall on their lives or, failing that, praying that they'd find the strength to muddle through.

"In the end," he told one man and his wife, "the strength to stand the hard times is a more valuable commodity than good times themselves."

"Brother Joe," the man said, "I'm fifty-three years old, and as late as four or five years ago, I would've said, 'Yeah, strength is more valuable.' But right now, I guess I'd take some good times over a key to the Pearly Gates."

For Aikman himself the times were not easy. He loved his job, he believed he was doing something important. But the insurance coverage offered by the church was inadequate for a man with two kids, one of whom had asthma. Jack was allergic to the defoliant the farmers sprayed on cotton, and it seemed like he spent half his time in the doctor's office. Tony needed fillings, and since they didn't have any dental coverage, Aikman had to pay out of his pocket. His car, a ten-year-old Honda, developed steering problems. Replacing the rack-and-pinion cost him seven hundred dollars.

One night, when he was sitting up late at the kitchen table, making notes for inclusion in the church bulletin, he heard Sally's slippers on the linoleum. Usually she went to bed as soon as the boys were asleep.

"Up late, aren't you?" he said.

She didn't answer. She walked over to the sink, turned on the tap, and filled a glass with water.

He was a better than average Bible scholar. He could have quoted any number of verses dealing with anger and the importance of controlling it. But just now they slipped his mind. What filled his head was an image from last night. He'd gone to bed early. He'd crawled in beside Sally and kissed her, and she'd kissed him back, and though at first she was anything but eager, she'd eventually begun to want him. He went at her with teenaged greed. But at a certain point she fell still, and when he looked down at her face, tears streaked it. "What is it?" he said, and she said, "There's almost nothing left in the checkbook."

Now, as she stood at the sink with her back to him, he said,

"I just asked you a harmless question. Are you deaf or what?"

"No," she said, "I'm not. But sometimes I wish I was. That and blind too."

"If you really had a handicap to deal with, you wouldn't say that kind of crap."

"I do have a handicap," she said. "My handicap's you. Most women have husbands that are willing to fix a leaky faucet or a clogged drain. I've got a husband that's willing to fix the world."

Pat had prepared the dinner herself. Pork roast with peppercorn mustard crust and cider gravy, onion and leek strudel, braised baby carrots. She looked across the table at Aikman: he eyed his plate as if he'd like to dive into it. But Sally stared at it with a strange expression. The food might have been wax, for all the appetite she displayed.

"Well," Pat said, "Brother Joe?"

Aikman said grace, and while he did it Pat watched him. He prayed intently, eyes squeezed shut, his face bathed in soft light from the chandelier.

He looked almost helpless. She had seen enough of him and his wife together to know something was badly wrong between them, though she wasn't sure what.

During the meal she tried to talk to Sally, but she could scarcely buy replies.

"What did you major in at Alabama?"

"Business."

"I thought about that too, but I don't know, I went ahead and studied French. I don't think I ever made better than a B+ on any of my papers."

"I made C's."

"Well, I made some of those too."

"What sorority were you in?"

"I wasn't in one."

At least Sally looked at her then. "I would have guessed otherwise," she said.

Pat lifted her glass and sipped iced tea. "I wasn't interested in sororities."

"I was," Sally said. "I just couldn't afford to belong."

Pat felt like she'd had her face slapped. It was a feeling she'd experienced before, when Nick had made her invite couples over. Sooner or later, the women would remind her that she was qualitatively different from them.

"I couldn't afford it either," she said. "My daddy was a bus driver. I was at Vanderbilt on a scholarship, and it didn't cover sorority fees."

Nick had tuned in. "Good thing it didn't," he said. "If you'd been a Tri-Delt, somebody would've snapped you up before I ever had a chance to lay eyes on you."

He reached across the table to squeeze her hand. Last night in bed he had squeezed her too, had grabbed a hunk of her flank and, grinning, pronounced her prime. Time had not changed the way he looked at her. She might still have been twenty-one, lying naked on a bed in the Holiday Inn. She knew a lot of women would feel grateful if their husbands looked at them that way. But the years had changed her: she was heavier now, in body as well as spirit. Her hair had begun to gray at the roots, and her days were gray too. If he couldn't see these changes, he couldn't see her.

For one awful instant, as his hand moved across the table toward hers, she believed she would stab him in the palm with her fork.

In January the church organist checked into Washington Regional in Greenville for removal of an ovarian cyst. Aikman planned to visit her the day after her surgery, but when he went out to crank his car that morning, it wouldn't start.

He looked across the yard. Sally stood at the kitchen window, staring at him and shaking her head. Rather than go back in and face her, he wrapped his muffler around his neck and started walking.

It was four miles to church. A couple of times people from his congregation stopped and offered him a ride, but he said he was out getting his exercise.

In his study, he doffed his coat and picked up the phone. Pat answered on the second ring.

"Hi," he said, "this is Brother Joe. You aren't planning to go see Sister Linda today, are you?"

"Why?"

"Well, I was intending to visit her, but something's wrong with my car. I thought if you were going, you might give me a ride."

She didn't hesitate. "I'd be happy to," she said.

She picked him up in the church parking lot. It was hot in the Volvo. Every encounter he'd ever had with her had occurred in a warm setting. He could not associate her with the cold.

Lately he thought about her often. Sometimes, when he was sitting alone in his study, he imagined slipping off with her somewhere. Not to a motel room, where he might moan over her and satisfy a need that he knew would reassert itself, with a vengeance, in an hour; but someplace bright and sunny—a park bench, say, on a nice spring day, or a row boat in the middle of a lake. He did not know what he'd say to her. Maybe he wouldn't say a word. Maybe he'd just row the boat or sit on the bench, and that would be enough.

She put the car in gear and turned into the road. "How'd you get to the church?" she said.

"Walked."

"You're joking."

"I'm an old athlete."

"It's four miles."

"Coach Bryant used to make us run five to warm up."

"Next time, call Nick or me. We're both up early."

"It's a deal."

In the car she was fast and reckless, just as he'd expected. She passed everything, including a highway patrolman who, for whatever reason, elected not to pull her over. They got to Greenville in twenty minutes.

They spent an hour with Linda. Before they left, Aikman knelt and prayed for her recovery. On the way back, Pat asked if he had time for her to run into Kroger and buy a few things off her grocery list.

He pushed the basket while she pulled items from the shelf. She said it felt strange to go shopping with a man. Nick had never accompanied her, not once in all these years.

"I used to do all the shopping for us," Aikman said.

"Sally's lucky."

"That'd be news to her."

She stopped and looked at him. "Really?"

Rather than reply to her question, he said, "I worked in a grocery store before I went to the seminary. I can walk in one anywhere in the country and tell a lot about the manager in five minutes."

"So tell me what you know about whoever runs this one."

"He's cautious. You don't see a lot of items double-stacked, which means he doesn't risk big orders—if he did, he'd get the stuff out here, because you don't let it sit in the back room a day longer than you have to. Also, he's got a very orderly mind. Everything's fronted—see how all the labels are facing out?"

"I hadn't noticed that, but you're right."

"He's probably a good guy to work for, until you make a mistake. The first time you mess up, he'll correct you gently. The second time, you're gone." He forced himself to grin. "My boss is a little more forgiving."

They were standing in the middle of an aisle, next to a Gatorade display. She said, "Don't you think your boss is a lot more forgiving?"

"Yeah, I do," he said. "But sometimes I worry about pushing my boss too far."

"You think that's possible?"

"Not really, but I'm scared to find out."

He carried her groceries out to the car. She cranked up. "You don't drink," she said, "do you?"

"Why?"

"Well, since you smoke, I thought maybe you aren't averse to a drink too, and if you're not, I'd suggest we stop and have one."

He looked at his watch. "It's just twelve-thirty. Isn't that a little early?"

"I think bars open at lunch."

"It's a bar you had in mind?"

"That's the normal place to get a drink, isn't it?"

Watching her, he noticed how her hands had tightened on the wheel. His reluctance had made her angry or frustrated or—more than likely—both.

If someone from Indianola stopped off at a Greenville bar and observed him parked at a table, enjoying a drink with Nick Dodd's wife, his troubles would at last be complete. But for just a second—which after all, he reflected later, would be long enough for Jesus Christ to split the sky and sweep this world away—he didn't care one bit.

They settled on a place called the Cotton Patch. It was far enough off Highway 82 that nobody they knew was likely to appear. When they walked in, the only person there was the bartender, a weathered blonde of indeterminate age; she was watching a soap opera. They ordered Miller Lites and took a table in the corner.

Pat almost never used alcohol. She'd tried it at parties in college, and she'd learned she couldn't handle it. Today, after two swallows, her head began to feel cloudy. "You know what?" she said.

"What?"

"I hate beer."

"I thought you wanted a drink."

"I guess I should've ordered something in a tall glass with lots of fruit flavors and crushed ice."

"I don't think they serve that at this kind of place. I believe this is just beer and nothing else."

"How can you tell?"

"You just can," he said. "You haven't been in a bar before, have you?"

"Does it show?"

"A little bit."

"I guess there are a lot of things I haven't done."

"There are a lot of things I haven't done too," he said. "And I've done a few things I wish I hadn't."

"Like what?"

"For instance," he said. "Back in high school we were playing a team from Jasper, Alabama, for the state title. I got up to the line on fourth down and didn't recognize the defense they were in and called time-out. But we didn't have any time-outs left, so we got slapped with a five yard delay-of-game penalty, and when we finally did run the play, we came up two yards short of the first down. I still wish I hadn't called that time-out."

He was grinning at her, as if to show her that he didn't really regret it or worry over it anymore, but she refused to let it end there. "What choice did you have?" she said. "You didn't know what you were facing. You just got confused, that's all."

He studied the tablecloth, a sheet of black vinyl. She guessed she'd finally made him uncomfortable. She drank a little more, lit a cigarette and took a puff. "Shit," she said.

"What's the matter?" he said. "Something got you down?"

"I guess so."

"Life, maybe?"

"Something like that."

"Want to talk about it?"

Mist marred her vision. "I can't talk about it—I'm not sure what's wrong with me."

"I'm not sure what's wrong with me either," he said. "So we're in the same boat."

When he said that, she knew what she wanted. With the frosted glass cold in her hands and Joe Aikman sitting two feet away, she had an urge to seize what wasn't hers. She let herself imagine Aikman's mouth at her breast. She did not know what she'd feel if he made love to her, but she believed she would finally feel something.

The bar was dark and dingy: countless stealthy pleasures

had been negotiated here, over cigarettes and beer. The place was too seamy for the words she wished to utter. She made a silly joke about leaking boats. She finished her beer, and Joe Aikman finished his.

In unison they glanced at their watches.

"Time to go?" he said.

"Absolutely."

The next Sunday, when Aikman surveyed his congregation, she was absent. Nick sat in his usual place, with both of their kids. Afterwards Aikman asked about Pat. Nick said she had the flu.

A couple of days later, as Aikman sat in his office composing his next sermon, he heard tires crunching gravel. He knew it was her.

He opened the door. Snow flurries swirled in the air. A stiff wind blew across the field on the other side of the parking lot. Yesterday the pipes in the parsonage had frozen, and the plumber who did cut-rate work for the church wouldn't be available for another two days. Sally was at home dirty and mad. There was no water for coffee. The toilet had backed up.

Pat's eyes were streaked with red. She walked past him, into the office. She pulled off her coat and her gloves and sat down.

Ever since the day he'd accompanied her to the bar, he'd been imagining this scene in his mind. She'd light up, her fingers trembling. She'd puff the cigarette, look first at her lap, then at a distant corner where no object of earthly interest resided. She'd cough and toy with the hem of her skirt.

I think I'm in love with you, she'd say. *I don't know for sure. I've never been in love before.*

Then, in a rush, he'd drag out all his secrets, like so much soiled linen. He'd tell her that his wife turned to stone when he touched her. He'd tell her that he and his whole family were about to go under. He'd say he didn't know what to do next or where to turn. Prayer, he'd confess, hadn't solved a thing.

And finally, he would admit that whenever he was around her, he thought about making love to her, that he thought about it too when she was nowhere in sight. *I like you*, he would say. *I like to be with you. I like to talk to you, I like the way you look, and I really want to hold you right now.*

She lit up, her fingers trembling. She puffed the cigarette and toyed with the hem of her skirt. He sat there in his swivel chair waiting for her to speak, and to keep from staring at her, he made himself look at the objects on his desk. There was a picture there of Sally and the boys sitting in the swing on his mother's back porch and, next to the picture, his Bible. His brass paperweight, which was shaped like praying hands, stood beside the telephone, and beneath that, in his desk drawer, were his sermons, every one he'd ever written, all the way back to his first year of seminary, each of them indexed according to theme. Faith, Charity, Forgiveness, Devotion.

*H*oe
Hands

Tea Burns was a lot older than the other hoe hands I chopped cotton with that summer. On his neck he had a goiter the size of a grapefruit, he had watery eyes and a crooked nose, but he claimed that in his youth he had been a handsome man. After he found out that I knew and loved the blues, he told me Bessie Smith had once sat in his lap on the porch of a little country store up close to Benoit.

"She had on a big-brimmed hat with a purple feather in it," he said. "She whispered something in my ear, but I ought not tell a young white boy what. She had a smell I won't never forget."

He owned an old Sears archtop that he kept in open tuning. He'd sit on the rickety steps of the tenant house he lived in, and he'd play slide guitar, wearing the neck of a Dr. Pepper bottle on his third finger and running it over the frets. It sounded a lot like Fred McDowell.

Grandpa said Tea was the best hoe hand he'd ever seen. He was a tall man with long legs and a long stride, and he set a stiff pace for the others. They were always telling him to slow down.

"He just bust ass to get to the turnrow," his wife, Rosie, would complain. "He act like it's Saturday and he's headed for town."

Her sister Essie Mae would hike up the cotton skirt she always wore over her khakis and mop the sweat beads from her face. "Sister," she'd say, "you married the kind of nigger that can't help but bring a smile to the white folks' face."

"White folks got Plymouths, Cadillacs, and Pontiacs," Tea would shoot back. "You want to ride to town, you better learn to make 'em smile, not frown."

Then they'd all glance over their shoulders at me. "It ain't you we talkin' about," Tea Burns would say. "So don't you get started sulking. Long as you're out here, you're one of us."

I knew he meant it as a compliment, but I also knew he knew it wasn't true. As Grandma liked to point out, I didn't have to be where I was that summer—in the middle of a cotton field, in one hundred–degree heat, with gnats in my ear—but Tea and Essie Mae and Rosie and the others did. I didn't live in a tar paper shack, use a slop jar to piss in, take a bath in a tin washtub. I hadn't gone to see Martin Luther King when he marched through the Delta, and I hadn't cried the night he died.

And though I could rip off a perfect T-Bone Walker run on the used Strat my Dad had bought me or play about as clean a Berry riff as you could ask for, I couldn't get that special rasp in my voice when I tried to bawl "Crossroads." Eric Clapton couldn't quite do it either. Neither one of us had ever dragged a 150–pound cotton sack a quarter of a mile with dust in our noses, the skin raw on our fingers where the cotton bolls had cut them.

Tea and Rosie and Essie Mae and all the others sounded like they had gravel in their throats. Along about five o'clock, somebody would start singing, soft at first, then louder. I'd quit chopping, I'd stop dead-still, lean on the hoe handle, let those voices wash over me.

Off toward Leland, the sun was burnt orange, hot as a big ball from hell. *I'm gone rest my tired sore body*, Rosie Burns wailed, *when I lay my burden down*.

I had gone to live with Grandma and Grandpa because Dad worked on a towboat and was away a lot, and Mother, who waited tables at a truck stop in Greenville, had fallen in love with another man. One Saturday night, Dad and I had come home from a Golden Gloves tournament and found a note taped to the refrigerator. It said that she was sorry, but she wouldn't be back.

Every night for the next few weeks I lay in bed in the empty apartment recalling how she used to let me sit in the kitchen at the truck stop and eat french fries while she carried four or five plates out at once, how she used to take me to the circus when it came through the Delta. We always sat at the end of the ring in the cheap seats, but that was a good place to be. When they had the tractor pull, the noise wasn't quite as bad down there.

I missed the feel of her hand on my face when she shook me awake in the mornings. I missed hearing her hum when she cooked, I missed helping her wash dishes. Every day I went home from school hoping she'd come back, but the only sound I heard when I opened the door was a creaking hinge, the kitchen clock ticking.

I wasn't leaving much when I left Greenville. But still I hated to go, because moving to my grandparents' place just outside Indianola cost me a spot in a pretty good band. There were four of us—two guitar players, a bass player and a drummer. We played three-chord blues and fifties rock and roll. Our drummer, the only one of us who lived in a single-family house, had a garage out back, and we'd get out there with the doors closed and rattle the walls. Sometimes his father would come out and yell at us to tone it down, but most of the time everybody left us alone. We played till our fingers were so sore we couldn't fret the strings. We once kept "Stormy Monday" going for an hour and a half nonstop.

We'd all listened to the British rock bands—the Stones, Cream, the Yardbirds, and John Mayall—and from there we'd gone back to their source. Which, as it turned out, was right here in the Delta. Fred McDowell was from Como, Jimmy Reed from Leland, and Charlie Patton had lived on the Heathman Plantation.

Our bass player, a fat kid named Norman whose mother had run off too, said, "Just imagine. Our granddaddies may have worked in the fields with one of those dudes and not even known they could play."

The drummer said, "Our great-granddaddies may have owned one of those dudes' granddaddies."

Norman said, "None of my granddaddies owned anybody. They didn't even own themselves."

The drummer said, "You owning up to being trash?"

I said, "As far as most folks are concerned, we're all trash."

The second I heard myself say it, I realized it was true. Norman and I lived in an apartment complex where somebody got evicted at least once a week. All the men who lived there were devoted to Miller Hi-Life, George Jones, and the Delta Motor Speedway. They worked at garages, they worked on barges, and policemen knew them on sight. The women were waitresses, convenience store clerks. After getting off work, they liked to drink beer in the bars along Highway 82. When they went to the drugstore to pick up a prescription, the pharmacist did not call them *Mrs.*, he used their first names. *Jenny Jones*, he would say. *Mary Wiggins*. Our mothers were no strangers to the Goodwill store.

Teachers assumed we wouldn't go to college. They urged us to take shop, so that like our fathers we could learn to repair enough engines to buy our nightly six-pack. They believed our Christmases were lacking in cheer, so for a couple of weeks each January they'd call on us in class and praise our efforts when we gave the wrong answers. Then they'd start noticing our long hair again and remember how much we loved rock and roll. They'd remember that in a year or two we'd be siphoning gas out of their tanks or maybe even trying to hot-wire their cars. Our names would be reentered on the shit-list.

There was a record store in the black part of town that sold records by Muddy Waters, Howlin' Wolf, Reed, McDowell, and a host of others. The four of us would meet on Saturday mornings and walk down there, past crumbling storefronts and muddy yards where black children played naked, using tin cans and old tires as toys.

We didn't buy anything at the record store. We didn't even go inside. We just hung around out front, listening to the records and all the black voices. At first, we drew some pretty strange looks, but after a while, people got used to seeing us there. A few days before Christmas the owner walked out of the store and gave each of us a couple of worn 45s.

"These done been played to death," he said. "See if you all can't get some use out of 'em."

We started trying to talk like black people ourselves. *Yes, suh,* we'd say. *She know she fine. Show do. Show nuff. Yes, Jesus.* Black people, we noticed, liked Colt 45, which we made up our minds to drink as soon as we were old enough to buy it. Norman got some sort of styling comb and tried to tease his hair into an afro. It worked pretty well except that he was blond.

The day I told the other guys I was moving, we talked a little about trying to keep me involved in the band, but we finally agreed it would be impossible. None of us was old enough to drive, and even if we had been, we didn't have cars or the money for gas.

Norman did his best to console me. "Indianola's a good place to go, though," he said. "That's where B. B. and Albert are from. You can probably get their records real easy over there."

Grandma and Grandpa didn't own a stereo, and if they had owned one, they would never have let me play records by blues artists on it. "If I want to hear niggers," Grandma liked to say, "all I've got to do is go to the field. But since I don't want to hear 'em, I stay home."

"A lot of good living at Indianola'll do me," I told Norman.

Having his mother run off had turned him into an optimist. He was the kind of kid who'd see an F on his report card and reason that it was just four letter grades away from an A.

"Well," he said, "you can't ever tell. You're liable to meet B. B. himself."

One Saturday morning at breakfast, while Grandpa was reading the Jackson paper and sipping his coffee, Grandma said, "When do you aim to talk to Tea about that old television set?"

She and Grandpa ran a small store on their place. The black families that worked for them bought most of their food there. Grandpa drove into town once or twice a month and filled up a couple of shopping carts with Vienna sausages, Red Bird potted meat, and Saltine crackers. He brought the stuff home, marked it up ten or fifteen cents, and stacked it on the shelves at the store. Grandma sold old clothes there, and whenever she bought a new appliance, she'd stand the old one on the store porch until one of the black people said, "Miz Lucille, how much you want for that clothes washer?" Tea and Rosie had bought an old black-and-white TV from her a few weeks back.

Grandpa lowered his paper. "How far behind are they?"

"Three weeks."

"How much are they supposed to pay a week?"

She wrinkled up her nose. A doctor had removed all the cartilage in it when he discovered a tumor there. Now she could mash it completely flat. "Five dollars," she said.

At that time you paid a good hoe hand four dollars a day. They worked from six in the morning till six in the evening, with an hour off at lunch. I did a little math in my head. Tea and Rosie were each making twenty dollars a week, twenty-four if they put in a whole day on Saturday. I only got paid two dollars a day, but I had trouble telling a cotton stalk from a stand of Johnson grass.

Grandpa said, "Let me finish my coffee and I'll go get on 'em about it."

He said it as if they were kids that kept weaseling out of their homework.

That afternoon he and Grandma rode into town to buy a load of stuff for the store. After they left, I grabbed the Strat and took off up the road.

Grandma had told me not to go to Tea's house. "It's too close to the road," she'd said. "People from the community drive by there, and if they see you messing around with colored folks, they'll wonder what kind of grandma I am." But every now and then, when I was pretty sure I wouldn't get caught, I'd go up there and beg him to teach me some licks.

His and Rosie's house was at the edge of the cotton field. A two-room shotgun, it had a tin roof. Tin siding had been nailed on three sides to keep the wind out. A handpump stood at one end of the porch.

Tea and Rosie had three kids. The oldest was about six or seven, the youngest just a baby. I knew them all by name. Most days they went to the field with us. The older ones played chase up and down the rows, hurling dirt clods at one another whenever the notion struck them. Rosie usually left the baby at the edge of the woods, in a Clorox box she'd covered with mosquito netting. Whenever we took a water break, she'd sit under a tree and nurse. Every time I'd been to their place before, the kids had been out in the yard, but today they were nowhere around.

Just as I decided they'd all gone to town, I heard Rosie's voice. "That bitch mess with me," she said from inside the house, "I'll go upside her head."

"Tell you one thing, girl," Tea said, "you better go over yonder, take a look in that mirror. Sound to me like you about to forget what you are."

"I ain't a what," she said. "I'm a who. I can't say the same thing for you."

There was a loud jolt, followed by the sound of breaking glass. It was a sound I knew well. I'd heard it pretty often around the apartment complex in Greenville. Sometimes the sound came from the room next to mine.

A second later, Rosie walked out the door, one hand clamped to her cheek. If she saw me, she didn't let on. I watched her walk down the steps, across the yard, and into the road. She didn't even have her shoes on.

Tea came out. He was wearing old khakis and a dingy undershirt. He opened his mouth like he intended to holler at Rosie. Then he saw me standing there with the guitar case in my hand.

"How you doin'?" he said.

For some reason my eyes had gotten wet. I felt as if I were melting from the inside out, and it didn't have anything to do with July heat.

"You wantin' me to sing some for you?" he said. "You wantin' to hear the lowdown blues?"

"I can come back later," I said.

"Ain't no need to do that," he said, turning, going into the house. "Tea got his old music box right here."

He was back in a second, with that sunburst Sears archtop. He sat down on the top step. I watched him slip the bottleneck onto his finger.

He hit a sliding note, ran it up to the twelfth fret and let it hang there quivering. "Remind you of a woman," he said, his eyes shut tight. "Woman been crying all night."

He pulled off, hit an open chord, then started a little four-note riff back down at the third fret. He played it five or six times. I knew he was making up some words.

Finally he threw back his head. A dark vein pulsed in the goiter.

I'm gone care my chair down to the river, gone sit and let them waves roll over me. Gone care my chair down to the big river, let them muddy waves roll over me. Gone let that cold dark water wash away Tea's misery.

He'd play five or six riffs while he made up the next verse. I took the Strat out of the case and sat down beside him on the steps.

A Strat's a solidbody, and you can't hear it very well unless you play it amplified. But I didn't need to hear it that day. Tea's foot stomped a beat on the step, rhythm ran up my feet and legs and into my hands and fingers.

I'm gone quit choppin' cotton, I'm gone steal me a car and go to town. Quit choppin' white folks' cotton, steal a long limousine and drive to town. Gone go to the Western Auto, swipe a gun and shoot my loudmouthed woman down.

He glanced at me, raised his eyebrow and nodded. It's a

gesture any musician in the world understands, and I understood it that day. But I couldn't think of any words to sing that would make any sense when they entered the air.

Monday morning, we went to the field on the back side of Grandpa's place. It was down close to the Sunflower River. Most of the land along the river was rich sandy land, but that field was buckshot. You call it that because a handful of it feels like the pellets in a shotgun shell. Grandpa never made a good crop on that land. Mostly it grew red vines, tea weeds, and cockleburs.

We were out in the middle of the field, hacking away at a stand of Johnson grass that must have been six feet tall, when I saw a dust cloud rising over the turnrow. When the dust settled, I could see Grandpa's pickup.

It was too early for a water break. I wondered if maybe my father hadn't been killed on the river—maybe they were coming to tell me. Or maybe Mother had come back and they intended to drive me home.

We got closer to the end of the rows, and the truck door opened and Grandma got out. She raised her hand to shade her eyes.

"That's Miz Lucille," Essie Mae said.

Grandma didn't come to the cotton field too often. She sat home shelling beans and peas and watching TV. It was Grandpa that hauled us water.

"Wonder what she want?" Rosie said.

"Look to me," Tea said, "like the lady mean business."

Rosie said, "Lady, my ass."

"Sister," Essie Mae said, "you better cool your fanny."

Right then I understood that on Saturday, when Rosie threatened to go upside the head of "that bitch," she was talking about Grandma. The possibility hadn't occurred to me before. I had never heard a black person call a white person names, though I'd been hearing the reverse all my life and considered it a normal thing.

"She fool with me," Rosie said, "I'm gone cool her fanny."

Gone jam her butt in that cold water can."

"Yes, Lord," said Tea, in a singsong voice, "I'm gone dip that lady in them good old cooling waters."

"Liable to stick your ass in there too."

"Indeed," said Tea. "Essie Mae, get ready to get in the road. Time your sister chill Miz Lucille, you and me'll be looking for lodging."

I risked a glance at Rosie's face. Her eyes had a glassy unfocused look.

We reached the turnrow. Grandma was standing near the pickup truck. She had her hands jammed into the pockets of her pants.

"Tea," she said, "you and Rosie are supposed to pay me five dollars a week for that TV set. You let yourselves fall three weeks behind. Mr. Henry says he talked to you about it Saturday."

"Yes, ma'am," Tea said. "He did. We give him nine dollars."

"Nine's not fifteen. I paid you all last Friday. Paid you and Rosie both twenty dollars apiece. I could've held out on you, but I didn't."

"No, ma'am," Tea said. "You didn't hold nothing out. Paid us both twenty dollars. That's right."

"What'd you all do with it?"

"We come down to the commissary Friday evening," Tea said. "Bought some food to feed the kids."

"Mr. Henry said you spent twelve dollars there. You paid me nine, so that's twenty-one. What happened to the other nineteen?"

Tea said, "We give a little at the church."

"Went to Indianola, I bet," Grandma said, "and pitched a big party down in the Quarters."

Rosie said, "I'd like to see you make do with what we get by on."

Grandma's lips quivered. "What'd you say?"

Rosie's daughter stood behind her, clinging to her leg. "Said I'd love to see you get by on so little," Rosie said.

"I've got by on a lot less," Grandma said. "The difference is I earned mine."

Rosie looked at her as if she'd just claimed to be the mother of Jesus or the queen of England. "Goddamn," she said, "how the living hell you think we come by ours?"

Grandma whirled. There were several hoes in the back of the pickup, their blades resting on the tailgate. She grabbed one of them.

Gripping the hoe with both hands, she turned on us. The blade looked razor-sharp, sunlight played on the silver gleaming edge.

Rosie pushed her daughter away. She lifted her hoe, took a single step toward Grandma.

Essie Mae said "Sister," and Tea said "Lord Jesus." I didn't say a word or move an inch. I felt like I'd taken root in the cotton field, like I'd never escape from that moment.

All the color drained out of Grandma's face. She lowered her hoe and did her best not to trip stepping backwards.

They left the place the next morning. I was sitting on the porch with the Strat on my knee when they went by in a pickup truck. I didn't know who the truck belonged to, but the man at the wheel looked familiar. Later on Grandpa told me the driver farmed land south of town. He'd paid off their debts, and from now on they'd be living on his place and working for him. In a year or two, I figured, he'd get mad at them, and they'd be in the road again. That was pretty much the way things worked in the Delta.

They weren't moving much furniture except a water-stained mattress and a chest of drawers. The archtop was wedged in between them.

I've always imagined Tea nodded at me as they rolled past, just as he'd nodded the day we played guitar on his porch. I imagine he was telling me to make up some words. About a family in a pickup, about dust and gnats and the Mississippi heat. The way sunlight flashes off the blade of a hoe. A woman crying all night.

I don't know if he nodded or not—I wasn't looking at him. I had my eyes on Rosie. She was sitting on the wheel well, the Clorox box resting on her lap. She had one arm around her daughter, one arm around her son. From the way her lips moved, I could tell that she was singing.

T^{he} Tower

My father was a farmer, but he didn't own land, just rented, and he didn't leave me much to start with except a pair of old Case tractors. After I left the navy, I tried farming for a while. I grew cotton on sixteenth-section land with my wife's father, but that didn't quite work out. He could find too many uses for turnrows. Mainly he liked to park his truck on them and hop in the back with a neighbor's wife and see if they couldn't wear his shocks out. I kept getting dragged into all the trouble he stirred up. Pretty soon I'd just had enough.

For a while I ran a cotton gin, then the price of cotton fell, and the owner sold the gin—they disassembled the son of a gun and put it on a boat bound for Egypt. I worked for Hillis Petroleum setting flame cultivators, I worked for the Indianola Compress and for Joe Breen Refrigeration. Then the price of cotton rose, and I ran a gin again. It was while I was doing that that I saw the correspondence course ad in an issue of *Popular Electronics*. I'd always been interested in radio and TV—I'd just barely failed the test for radar school in the navy—and I knew the state was about to start an educational television network, with a transmitter scheduled to be built somewhere near Indianola. It was a long shot, but I trained myself at night and passed the FCC exam. And eventually the network hired me.

For twenty-two years I got up twice a week at four in the morning and drove down to the transmitter. It stood out in the middle of a cotton field a few miles from town. It was just a small, flat-roofed brick building jammed with about two million dollars' worth of broadcast equipment. We picked up our signal from Jackson by microwave, then beamed it out

over an eighteen hundred–foot tower, the second tallest in the
state at that time. From the top, where I liked to go and my
boss, Marty Johnson, was scared to death to set foot, you could
see parts of three or four counties. On a good, clear day, you
might glimpse the Yazoo Hills.

It was my job to get the transmitter on the air and keep it
on the air until midnight. Every hour I'd make an entry in
the logbook, and every few minutes I'd flip a switch on the
wave-form monitor and check the test signals. I'd glance at
the tower light monitor occasionally and make sure all the
aircraft beacons were flashing. But mostly what I did was sit
in a swivel chair before the console and do my best to stay
awake. I read a lot of war novels, stuff by Jack Higgins and
Alistair MacLean. I read *The Eagle Has Landed* fifteen or twenty
times.

I took the job the year I turned forty, and I quit four years
ago, three weeks after my sixty-second birthday. Looking
back, I can see that of all the jobs I had, that job was the only
one I was really meant for. But when I was working there, if
you'd asked me if I liked it, I would have said no. Seven or
eight different men filled our third personnel slot down
through the years, and I got along well with almost all of
them. But I hated Marty Johnson. If I had all the money he
screwed me out of during those years, I'd be pissing in high
cotton now.

He was a thin little guy, about shoulder-high to me. He
had the face of a weasel. Talking to you, he'd always focus on
your ear or your forehead or maybe your adam's apple, but
he'd never look you in the eye. When he got up close, you
could smell something like beer on his breath. I know it wasn't
that, though, because Marty didn't drink. Alcohol gave him
headaches that almost struck him blind. He told me he hadn't
touched it since he left the service. That smell was the odor of
the fermentation going on in Marty Johnson.

He bought a new pickup every two or three years. He wore
designer jeans. In the summertime, he'd wear T-shirts with
the names of popular TV shows stenciled on them. He al-

ways wore a pair of good running shoes, but as far as I know he never ran.

He had his own desk, with an electric typewriter on it that neither me nor the third engineer was ever supposed to touch. A locked file cabinet stood beside the desk, and the day I went to work at the station, Marty told me not to ever open it. He said the paperwork inside it was only for the eyes of the station exec. If I messed with it, he said, he'd have my ass. I should've stuffed him in the damn file cabinet right then, but at the time the job meant the world to me. I wanted to send my daughter to college, so she wouldn't have to scrap and scrape like Marilyn and me, and that job paid me better than any job I'd ever had.

At best Marty was an awful on-site engineer. When anything major went wrong on his shift, he'd try to call me, and if I was gone or if I told Marilyn to say I wasn't home, he'd call Jackson. Kent Holden, the director of engineering for the network, would get on the phone and try to talk him through it, but more often than not, Kent or somebody else would have to jump in the car and pretend they were Richard Petty in a race to the Delta.

Through the network grapevine, I'd heard that Marty had gotten the job as station chief because he'd grown up in Tupelo, and he knew something damaging about the governor who was in office when the network started up. He'd kept the job because he knew something damaging about Kent Holden.

And I never got the job, even though I learned something damaging about Marty himself.

My wife was slim when I married her, but she gained a lot of weight back in the fifties, right after Stella was born, and she never did manage to get rid of it. For a few years she tried dieting, but she'd always break down late at night, and I'd hear her rummaging through the refrigerator. One evening, when she woke me up doing that, I staggered out of bed, needing to take a piss. As I walked by the kitchen, I looked in. She was standing at the refrigerator with the door open, forking lemon meringue pie into her mouth. Tears the size of gumdrops were rolling down her cheeks. I'd deviled her some about her weight, but after that night I didn't even mention it. We'd sat up a year's worth of evenings together, trying to balance a checkbook against impossible odds, and we'd seen the look on each other's faces when we both lost our minds in the mall down in Jackson and bought Stella some supertoy that folks like us just couldn't afford.

The day the first phone call came, Marilyn and I were sitting on the couch near the console. She was drinking a milk shake—she'd bought lunch at the Dairy Queen and driven down to eat with me. It was the fall of '79. I know that because Stella had just graduated from Ole Miss, gotten married, and moved out West, and we were sitting there talking about trying to get together enough money to go see her, when the phone near the console rang. It was the regular phone, not the red one network headquarters used when they needed to talk to us.

I reached over and picked it up. I figured it was probably somebody wanting to know what time *Austin City Limits* would be on that evening.

"WKIA," I said.

The voice on the other end was soft and low and smooth— Jack Higgins might have called it seductive. "May I speak to Marty Johnson?"

"He's off today," I said. I knew it wasn't June, Marty's wife. Her voice sounded like a cotton gin warming up.

"Do you know when he'll be in?"

"He's working Mondays and Wednesdays this month. I can give you his home phone number if you want it."

"That's all right," the voice said, "I'll try to reach him on Monday."

The connection broke. That was all. No goodbye, no explanation, no nothing.

I told Marilyn about it. She stirred her milk shake with her straw. "Maybe Marty's got himself a girlfriend," she said.

I laughed out loud. "That little weasel? Fancy pants and jogging shoes are not that big a draw. Plus he'd be too scared of June to mess around."

"Maybe she wouldn't care."

"Meaning what?"

"Maybe she's got somebody else herself."

"Is that what you've heard?"

"Well, there's been rumors going around."

"And you haven't told me?"

"I feel bad about telling you now."

"Do it anyhow."

"Well, a couple of folks have told me she's seeing a fellow that works for Delta Chemical."

I found that hard to believe. There was something harsh about June, and it wasn't just the sound of her voice. She had a square jaw, gunmetal gray hair that she'd always worn short, and nobody that I knew of had ever seen the woman in a dress. Most men, I believed, wouldn't find her very attractive, though for some reason I always had. She had an iron core, I thought, and I sometimes wished I had one too.

"Whether she's got somebody else or not," I said, "you can bet she keeps her little fox terrier on a mighty tight leash."

"Even a dog on a tight leash can get in trouble," Marilyn said, "provided the person holding the leash has got her eyes on something else."

We went back to talking about visiting Stella. But later, after Marilyn left, I started thinking about that damn phone call again. It'd be just like Marty Johnson to have something extra going on. He didn't have much to his credit as far as I could see, yet his accounts were always full. He'd been to the governor's mansion, he'd gone sailing on the Gulf with Kent Holden and the network chief. This year he'd gotten a six percent raise from the state for the second year in a row, while I hadn't come by an extra penny. Part of the reason was he'd written an evaluation of me that said, "Art Stucky is a good, solid technician" but "not a team player." He'd taken off three weeks a few months ago to go to Memphis for surgery on his back, and he told Kent Holden I'd complained about pulling his shift and mine. What I'd said when he came back was "I'm tired as a dog." It was a statement of fact, not a complaint.

He walked in about four that afternoon. He did that fairly often. He called his little visits "spot checks."

"Hey, Art," he said. "Looks like everything's tip-top, what with you being awake and all."

His hair was slicked down, it glowed beneath the overhead lights. He stood by his desk, leafing through the mail. He picked one envelope up, stared at it a minute, then crammed it into his side pocket.

I opened the logbook and started making my entry. "By the way," I said, "you got a phone call today."

"Yeah?"

"Yeah."

I wrote as slow as I could. *15:00-15:59 The World at War. 15:59-16:00 Station Break.*

"Well?" Marty said.

"Well what?"

"Was it Jimmy Carter or Billy Graham?"

"Actually," I said, "it was somebody I doubt either one of those two folks would have much use for."

"Like who?"

"Sounded like somebody from Las Vegas. Maybe one of those women that deals blackjack."

"I don't know how you'd know what a Las Vegas blackjack dealer sounds like," he said. "Every time you and Marilyn get a vacation, you head for someplace like Lookout Mountain or the Guntersville Caverns." He sounded spiteful enough when he said it, but there was a tremor in his voice that I usually heard only on the phone, when a aircraft beacon had gone out on his shift and he wanted me to jump in the pickup truck and come climb the tower.

"We go where we can afford," I said. "A junior engineer makes a lot less than a chief engineer. Just in case you didn't know it."

"I know it real well," he said. "I'm the man that hands out the checks." The grin he flashed me was too large for his face.

After he left, I sat in the swivel chair for a while, then got up and walked around. I went over to the kitchen area, put some water on to boil, then changed my mind and turned it off. Finally I opened the door and went outside.

I remember that the day was cool and hazy. I could hear a cotton picker grinding somewhere and over it the roar of the old Indianola Gin. The odor of lint hung in the air.

A television tower looks tall and narrow when you see it from a distance. But they're actually massive things. Imagine a three-sided steel triangle seven feet across each face, weighing two million pounds and anchored in a twenty-by-twenty-foot concrete slab. Twenty-seven guy wires—nine at each corner—maintain constant tension on the tower. Those wires are up to half a mile long and as thick as the thighs of a sumo wrestler. You set the tension on them with hydraulic pull jacks and strain gauges.

A chain link fence, six feet tall, surrounded our tower. I walked over and unlocked the gate, then closed it and locked it again from inside.

You can't tell it when you're driving by in a car, but television towers have tiny elevators in them. The elevator ascends through the center shaft. You have to go up the tower from time to time to change the bulbs on the side-lights or replace the ones in those flashing beacons, which are bolted to platforms that jut out from the tower. Our elevator was a steel-mesh cage big enough for two men. It would take you up to the very top, where the antenna was anchored. Only tower riggers—the folks who erect and maintain towers—could advance beyond that point.

I climbed into the elevator and pressed the button. Gears groaned, cables creaked, and the carriage started moving.

It's a funny feeling when the ground falls away, even if you're just sitting in an airplane. But I've been in planes taking off—we fly out to California once a year to see Stella and the grandkids—and it's not quite the same as going up the tower. Things on the ground get little fast when you're in a plane, until finally they just disappear beneath the clouds. That elevator only climbed about twenty feet per minute, which meant it took more than an hour to get to the top. And when you're moving upward that slow, you're never aware that what's on the ground is shrinking. It's almost like it's you that's changing, not just your relationship to what you're looking at.

That day I went up about a thousand feet. Off to the right, Indianola, which to begin with was just a bunch of green trees on the horizon, gradually took shape. I could see the gin spewing lint into the air. I could see the Academy, the all-white private school. We'd mortgaged our house to send Stella there, hoping, I guess, to convince her and ourselves that we were somehow better than the folks that sent their kids to Aaron Henry High. I could see the cars parked before Planter's Bank and Trust, which owned most of what I called mine. And I could see Marty Johnson's house. At first a stand of pecan trees hid it, then it came into view. It was twice as big as the little cabinet Marilyn and I made do with, but from up here it looked like a matchbox.

Finally I stopped the elevator, right next to a beacon platform. To reach the aircraft beacon, you had to slide open the elevator door, lean out, grasp the tower frame, and step across twenty-four inches' worth of no tomorrows. The platform itself was fifty-five inches long and thirty-one inches wide, a steel plate a quarter-inch thick. The beacon was bolted to the surface. There are a lot of private planes in the Delta, and because the land's so flat, pilots feel free to fly low. Those beacons were there to warn them something tall was in the way. When the bulbs inside the beacons went bad, they had to be changed immediately. To do that, you had to squat on the platform, unscrew a heavy bolt and a wing-nut, and raise the beacon's tinted cover. I'd replaced bulbs in every beacon on the tower. I didn't use a safety harness when I was out there on those platforms, though the rules said I had to. I didn't need one. I never felt dizzy or lightheaded.

I stood there several minutes, a thousand-foot drop just inches away, wind whipping through the tower, the elevator shuddering. I was thinking that up here, on the tower, it didn't matter who you knew or what you knew about them. It didn't matter whether you were the station chief or a junior engineer. It didn't matter if you'd ever seen the inside of a country club or been to Las Vegas. The age of your pickup didn't matter, nor did the size of the house you parked the pickup at.

Up here, on the tower, only one thing mattered, and that was where you put your foot.

It's odd the way memory works. I was on a light cruiser that took a Japanese torpedo to the bow one day over in the Coral Sea. A fireball shot about two hundred feet into the air, and before we stopped taking on water, several compartments had been flooded, including the brig, where fifteen POWs drowned.

As chief water tender, I was down in the engine room when the ruckus took place. The first thing I did was send the men up the escape trunk, then I secured the quick closing fuel line to shut off the oil and I closed off the steam lines. After that, I figured it was time to see if maybe I couldn't get out alive. I took off up the trunk, which was a vertical shaft thirty-three inches square. The temperature inside it was about 120 degrees. Normally it was lit, but the forward generators had been knocked out, so I climbed to the top in black darkness. Every time I passed through a deck-level, I had to push up a manhole cover that weighed close to forty pounds. I guarantee you I was scared, but that's not really what I remember. What I remember is that for some reason, the shaft smelled like a pizza that day. I don't know where the odor came from, but it was there, and I remember that as I climbed out, my goddamn mouth was watering.

And I remember it was sleeting the day the second of those phone calls for Marty Johnson came. When you're sitting under an eighteen hundred–foot tower, you tend to take an interest in anything that's got to do with falling ice. The stuff sticks to the tower, and when the temperature gets up above freezing, the ice starts letting go. I've seen chunks come crashing down that must have weighed thirty or forty pounds. Every year or two we'd have to repair damage to the roof.

The second call came about six weeks after the first one. The same woman again, no question about that.

"May I speak to Marty Johnson?"

"I'm sorry," I said, "he's not here. Can I take a message?"

"Just a moment," she said. It sounded like she'd muffled the phone and was asking somebody something. Then she said, "Do you have something to write with?"

"Sure."

"Please tell Mr. Johnson to call 901-221-9807 as soon as possible. He should ask for Patricia Gambrell."

"If it's something urgent," I said, "you can call him at home. He's in the Indianola phone book, or I can just give you the number now."

"Please just give him the message," she said. She hung up before I could say anything else.

I dialed his home phone, but nobody answered, so I wrote him a note and tacked it to the bulletin board. And then, without stopping to wonder why I was doing it, I copied down the number and the woman's name a second time and put the slip in my wallet.

I got home after midnight. Marilyn had long since gone to bed, but she opened her eyes when I crawled in beside her. I said, "There's been another one of those phone calls for Marty."

"What phone calls?"

I reminded her about the woman with the velvet voice.

She sounded groggy. "The one we thought might be his sweetheart?"

"Yeah," I said. "But this time it sounded like business."

"Business," she mumbled, "doesn't always rule out pleasure."

"She gave me a number for him to call. Long distance. Area

code 901. That's western Tennessee."

"Didn't he have that back surgery up in Memphis?"

"Yeah."

"Maybe it was his doctor's office calling. I bet that's what it was."

"Maybe so," I said, "but then why don't they want to phone him at home? That doesn't make any sense, does it?"

But Marilyn didn't answer. She'd already gone back to sleep.

I never would have learned any more than that if I hadn't written to Kent Holden, the chief of engineering for the network, to protest Marty's evaluation of me. I used some pretty strong language in my letter, and I said a thing or two about how I'd taken on a lot of responsibilities that I believed were not mine. I mentioned a couple of specific times when Marty had called me in to work on his shift, to fix something he either didn't know how to fix or was scared to fix. Under the circumstances, I said, I thought his comments about me not being a team player were pretty damned unfair.

Kent called me at the station one morning a few days before Christmas and said he was driving up to have a little chat about my letter. He showed up around two o'clock. He walked in and sat down on the couch and clasped his hands behind his neck. He wore a little black moustache that always looked as if he'd waxed it.

"Art," he said, "you're getting to be a smartass."

Kent grew up in a big house in a ritzy part of Jackson. His father, so I'd heard, had been a vice-president at Deposit Guarantee. Folks like that don't like to be challenged. For most of my life I'd behaved just like they wanted me to. They owned the gins I'd run, and when they told me how sorry they were that they couldn't pay me more, I always just nodded and claimed I understood. They ran the banks I borrowed money from. When they told me why they couldn't loan me quite as much as I needed, I always claimed I understood that too. But the truth was that I didn't understand, had never understood why folks who had so much were so goddamned unwilling to part with so little. Now that my daughter was out of college and on her own, I felt like I could be a lot less compliant. All I stood to lose was all I had, and I figured it wasn't enough to worry about.

I leaned back in my swivel chair and crossed my legs. "Better to be a smartass," I said, "than a dumb one."

A muscle started twitching near the corner of his moustache. "Are you calling me a dumbass?"

"Absolutely not," I said. "First off, I don't think you are one. And even if I did, I wouldn't call you that. It's childish to toss insults around, not to mention unkind."

"Are you calling Marty a dumbass?"

"No," I said, "I actually think that in a lot of ways, Marty's pretty damned smart. He happens not to know beans about running a TV transmitter, but that's not the only kind of knowledge worth having." I almost added that I'd like to know some of the stuff Marty knew. Word was, he'd attended a meeting in New Orleans a few years ago with Kent and caught him doing something he shouldn't have.

"That's a pretty sharp charge to make, Art," Kent said. "You're not offering any proof, though."

"I offered you proof in my letter."

"What you offered in your letter," Kent said, "was a bunch of anecdotes, all of which just proved to me that Marty's acting like a station chief should. He's in charge here. He's got the power to delegate responsibility."

"Has he got the power to order me to risk my life, time after time, on that tower? He's never set foot on it. Not once."

"I'll say it again. He's the station chief. He's got the power to do what he sees fit. You're the number-two man at this site—not number one. I'm beginning to understand what he means about you not being a team player."

He pulled a pack of cigarettes from his pocket, tapped one out, and lit up. "I admit," he said, "that sometimes the guy can be a bit abrupt."

I could just imagine Marty sitting next to Kent in some French Quarter bar. *By the way*, he'd say, *about that little sweet-*

meat you brought home last night? You needn't worry that I might spill your secret. How about a double raise next year—you can just give me mine and Art Stucky's too.

"The thing I've learned about Marty," Kent said, "is that he's got his generous side."

Actually, just give me my raise and two-thirds of Art's and you can keep the rest.

"It'd probably surprise you to know that when Marty took off to have his back operated on," Kent went on, blowing smoke rings at the ceiling, "he refused to bill it to his group insurance policy. Said he didn't want to do anything that might drive up our insurance costs. He said he was worried that if premiums rose any higher, the network might have to ask you guys to pick up part of your health insurance coverage and some of the junior engineers like you would be strapped."

"If he didn't bill it to his group insurance," I said, "who did he bill it to?"

"Said he had some private coverage that'd take care of it."

"I don't reckon he let you pay him sick leave, either?"

"You're damn straight we paid him sick leave. He's entitled to it, just like you are." He'd smoked his cigarette down to the nub. "I'm here to tell you something, Art," he said. "You're a good technician, one of the best we've got. But if you ever write me another letter like that again, you're gone. And the number of people looking to hire fifty-three-year-old transmitter technicians is pretty damn small. There're more folks eager to take a fiery poker up the ass."

He stood up, threw his coat on, and stalked out, looking pleased about getting off such a witty parting shot.

But the business about Marty charging his surgery to a private insurance policy had set me thinking. I didn't doubt that he had such a policy, but I didn't believe for one minute that he'd risk billing his own policy rather than the state's group insurance—and drive up his own premiums in the process—because he was worried about the welfare of people like me. He'd have to have a better reason than that. And whatever that reason was, I knew it was connected to those phone calls he'd been getting.

I had the next day off. Marilyn was working at Sunflower Food Store back then, and she didn't have to go on shift until eleven. I waited until she left the house, then I walked into the hallway, where the telephone was.

I'd thought some the previous night about what I aimed to do. It was not the kind of thing I'd ever done before. At one time in my life, right after that first gin shut down and let me go, I went through a couple of months where I spent too much time sitting on a bar stool at the VFW. I came home drunk once or twice and started a fight, acted nasty to Marilyn and Stella both. At another time, back when I was working for Joe Breen Refrigeration, I got a little too interested in the woman who did Joe's bookkeeping. She was divorced and had two kids, one of which was always on the verge of going to jail. One day, when I saw her standing by the window with a misty look in her eyes, I walked over to her, and before I knew what I was doing, I put my arm around her. She shut her eyes and leaned against me. "Sometimes," she said, "I'd like to be made out of metal." That was all it ever amounted to, I never did crawl off to Leland or Greenville and take her to a motel, though I can't say the thought never crossed my mind. What I can say is that while I had a lot of little flaws that might have become big ones, I'd never in my life been a sneak.

But that day I did something sneaky. Marty Johnson knew too much about too many people, I'd decided. It was time somebody learned a little more about him.

I removed that slip of paper from my wallet, I picked up the receiver, and I dialed that Memphis number. The woman that answered was the one I'd talked to before. "Dr. Kilgore's office," she said. "May I help you?"

Marty's voice was a little bit higher than mine, but otherwise I figured we sounded pretty much alike on the phone. "Yes," I said. "I'd like to speak to Patricia Gambrell."

"May I tell her who's calling?"

"This is Marty Johnson."

She put me on hold. My face had started sweating. Technically, I supposed, this was wire fraud.

"Mr. Johnson?"

"Yes."

"This is Patricia Gambrell."

"Good morning," I said.

"Mr. Johnson," she said, "I'm afraid what you proposed the other day just won't wash."

"I see," I said.

"We don't want to turn the account over for collection," she said. "I hope you understand that."

"Of course."

"If you remember," she said, "at the outset Dr. Kilgore advised you to try counseling, rather than insisting right away on the procedure. I believe he also warned you that in all likelihood your State Farm policy wouldn't cover the implant."

"That's true," I said. My pulse rate sped up.

"Mr. Johnson," she said, "we've tried to respect your request not to call you at home. We understand how sensitive these things can be when another person's feelings are involved. But once your account's transferred, what happens next is out of our hands."

"Well," I said, "you've done all you could. It was damn successful surgery. I thought you and the doctor might like to know that."

Patricia Gambrell's voice softened—you could tell she was an awfully nice woman. "That's wonderful," she said. "I'm happy for you, Mr. Johnson. I really and truly am."

After hanging up, I went out and got in my pickup and drove down to the public library. They've got the phone books for most major cities. I picked up the one for Memphis and started flipping through the yellow pages. It didn't take me long to find the entry, and when I found it, it said exactly what I'd thought it would.

Dr. J. K. Kilgore, the listing said. *Board Certified for the Practice of Urology.*

————

To get sick leave for more than three consecutive duty days, we always had to fill out a request and have it approved down in Jackson. At the very least, Marty was guilty of submitting falsified forms. Of course, you could always argue that the personal nature of the surgery had led him to lie, which I'm sure it had. But he could have gone on unpaid leave if he didn't want to tell the truth about the surgery. He'd obtained state money under false pretenses, and that wasn't the sort of thing the network accounting department could afford to ignore. Especially since we had a new governor who'd promised to stamp out corruption in state agencies.

I couldn't decide what to do with what I knew. On the one hand, I wanted to even my accounts with Marty Johnson, and if I turned him in, he'd most likely be gone. I might even end up as station chief. On the other hand, I'd already stooped to his tactics, and I hated for anybody—even Marty and certainly Marilyn—to know I had that in me. I hadn't known it myself until I did it.

So as Christmas approached, I was in a quandary. I had discovered that having leverage over somebody wasn't all that pleasant. There's something about being on the bottom looking up that's a lot more wholesome than being on the top looking down.

On the evening of the twenty-second, I went out to buy a bottle of wine for flavoring a stew Marilyn was cooking. Marty and June's house was just a few blocks from the liquor store, and I had to drive past it. He was on shift that night, but her Ford Galaxy stood parked in the drive.

A few days ago Marilyn had told me the guy June was supposed to be seeing had left town. Apparently he'd gotten a better job somewhere, or maybe he'd just wanted to break things off, if, in fact, there was anything to break off.

The curtains in the bay window were closed, but there was a light on in the living room. They didn't put up a Christmas tree anymore. Like Stella, both of their kids had gotten married and left the state.

I'd always liked June, so I thought, *What the hell, why not wish her Merry Christmas.* I parked on the street and walked across the yard.

She answered the door in a ragged pink bathrobe. Dark bags hung under her eyes. She looked like she'd either been drunk or asleep, I couldn't say which. Maybe both.

"Hi," I said. I was embarrassed. "I was driving to the liquor store and I saw your car. I just intended to wish you Merry Christmas."

She stared at me as if she was trying to bring my features into focus. There was a stain on the front of her robe. Coffee or Coke, something brown. "Oh, Art," she said, in that grating voice, "that's sweet of you."

"Well," I said, "Merry Christmas."

"Merry Christmas to you too."

"Thanks. Good night, June."

"Art?"

She stepped out into the yard. She was barefoot, I noticed, and the temperature had already dropped below freezing.

"Yeah?" I said.

She hugged herself. Her teeth must have been chattering. "Tell Marilyn Merry Christmas too."

"Sure," I said. "Take care of yourself, June."

She was still standing there hugging herself when I drove away.

I worked the twenty-third but had Christmas Eve off. Marilyn and I talked to Stella and our son-in-law for over an hour that night, then we sat down and ate a big turkey supper, cleared away the dishes, and got ready to open some gifts.

We'd just sat down beside the tree when the telephone rang. I wouldn't have answered it if I hadn't thought it might be Stella calling back.

It was Marty. "Listen," he said. "We've got a problem. You need to get down here quick."

My hand tightened up on the receiver. "What kind of problem?" I said.

"We don't have time to jaw," he said. "Just get on down

here right now." He hung up before I could say a word. I took the phone off the hook and walked back into the living room.

I told Marilyn what he'd wanted. "I'm going down there," I said, "but not till we've opened our presents."

"Let old Ebenezer sit and stew."

"Exactly."

So we busted open the packages. I'd bought her some new leather gloves and a muffler and a pair of house shoes, as well as a dress I'd seen her admiring in the window down at Kenwin's. She gave me some heavy-duty pruning sheers, a new Jack Higgins war novel, and a bottle of Jack Daniel's. It's not the same at Christmas after the kids leave home, but for us it's never been bad.

We put the presents away and cleaned up the paper and ribbons. Then I did what I'd done so often in the past. I put on my coat and my work shoes, and I walked outside, on what was supposedly my night off, and I got in the truck and cranked up.

It had rained the day before, and sometime last night the rain had briefly turned to ice. The temperature had climbed a degree or two above freezing around mid-afternoon, but the roads were still slick. I drove through town at about ten miles an hour. Everything had closed down, even the Mr. Quik. Only fools and Santa's elves were out this evening.

As soon as I cleared the city limits, I glanced off to the east out of habit. And I knew instantly what it was Marty Johnson wanted and why he hadn't told me on the phone.

When I walked in, he was standing by the console. He had both hands jammed in his pockets, and his face wore that hunted look it always had when something went wrong. He didn't even bother to insult me or ask what had taken me so long or bitch about the busy signal he'd gotten every time he dialed our number.

He pointed at the tower-light monitor. "It's that number-eight beacon," he said. "Both bulbs. We've got to tend to that sucker right now."

I knew what *we* meant. *We* meant *me*, unlucky Art Stucky.

I said, "Did you notify the FAA?"

"I didn't want to bother them. It's Christmas Eve."

"That's great," I said. "So somewhere up there, there's probably some little single-engine plane flying around for God knows what reason, and there's a holiday treat waiting for it at sixteen hundred feet. You beat all, you know that?"

He was twice as scared now. He'd violated procedure by not calling the FAA. He'd assumed there was no need to, because Art Stucky would come scale the tower. But I wasn't the same old Art, and I knew he wasn't the same old Marty Johnson. I'd shed a burden, my fear of losing my job. He'd gone to Memphis and come back with something new.

"Okay," I said. "You go on up and replace the bulbs, and I'll keep an eye on things here."

"You're the tower man," he said.

"You show me where it says that in my job description."

"I'm the station chief," he said. "I decide what your job entails. You get on out there now."

We were standing about two feet apart, and I could smell that yeasty odor rolling off him. He was trying his best to meet my gaze, but he couldn't quite do it. His eyes had honed in on my chin.

I opened my mouth to say, *Listen, you son of a bitch, you get out there on that tower or I'll grab your crotch and pump your rubber pecker through the ceiling.* I opened my mouth to say, *Okay, this does it, I'm calling Jackson and telling them you falsified sick leave, and this time next week I'll be the station chief.*

I opened my mouth and said, "Go get me the goddamn bulbs."

I had a screwdriver in my hip-pocket, a flashlight in my hand. Over my jacket I wore a hunting vest with baggy pockets. In each pocket I carried two six hundred–watt bulbs. The bulbs were the size of honeydew melons, and I only needed two, not four, but there was always the chance I'd drop one while I was out there on that platform. Especially on a night like this.

I knew there would be ice on the tower. The question was how much. I stood close to the elevator for three or four minutes, shining my flashlight up the tower, but I couldn't see anything but the guy wires coming off it. I got in and pushed the button.

Every time I exhaled, I'd puff a gray cloud out. It was dark most of the way up, but I'd pass a set of sidelights every hundred and fifty feet and a set of beacons every two hundred. The sidelights flooded the carriage with a harsh, white glow. The beacons flashed red like the lights on an ambulance.

At eight hundred feet I entered a patch of fog. For a few minutes, I couldn't see the tower frame, much less the ground. My toes were turning to ice, my hands were getting cold inside my leather gloves.

I came out of the fog at about nine hundred feet, and it was right after that that something hard bounced off the top of the elevator. I hit the button, stopped the carriage and listened. There wasn't much wind, just the whisper of a breeze. Aside from that, I couldn't hear a thing, so I went ahead and punched the button again.

I hadn't bothered to ask myself why I was doing this. I didn't ask myself why I was doing it when the carriage pulled level with the number-eight beacon and I tripped the latch on the elevator door. I didn't ask myself why I was doing it when, holding the flashlight in my right hand, I stuck my left foot over the threshold and reached out with my left hand, groping for that orange steel leg that formed the corner of the triangle.

My gloved hand felt a slick glaze, and the toe of my left shoe slipped. I pitched forward, flinging the flashlight away and hooking my right arm around the beacon.

Face down on a narrow platform sixteen hundred feet high, my cheek glued to a solid sheet of ice, my legs flopping out over nothing, I saw myself as Marty Johnson and Kent Holden and many others must have seen me. I was the soldier who scaled the wall first, I was the sailor who sank with his ship. I was the guy who always met his production quota but finally left his finger in a punch press. I had taken a lot of orders and eaten a lot of dirt in an effort to prove something to them and to myself.

Hugging the beacon now with both arms, I peeled my face off the ice and pulled my legs onto the platform. For several minutes I lay there, thinking of Marilyn and Stella and the grandchildren I expected to love in my old age. I would never tell them war stories, I promised myself. I would never tell them stories about battling stiff odds and coming out on top. I would never bitch about how hard a time I'd had. Instead I'd present my life to them as it presented itself to me in this moment.

It was basically uneventful, I'd tell them. *It wasn't always easy, but it was never impossible either.*

One night, I'd tell them, *more or less by accident, I added everything up, saw how precious my life was, and I've been holding on like crazy ever since.*

I sat up. I locked my legs around the beacon and reached into the pockets of the hunting vest. One bulb was intact, but I'd crushed the other three when I fell. If I hadn't been wearing a heavy jacket and a thick flannel shirt, the glass would probably have ended up piercing my stomach.

I took the screwdriver out of my pocket and began to chip away at the glaze on the beacon. I couldn't see a thing—I didn't need to. I had to work on the bolt and the wing-nut a while, but I managed to raise the hood. I unscrewed one of the bad bulbs and dropped it over the edge. When I screwed the new one in, the beacon began flashing.

I thought of Marty Johnson sitting in his swivel chair sixteen hundred feet below me, in a room that was well lit and warm. Watching the monitor on the wall, he'd see that number-eight light start blinking. He'd get up and walk away from the console. He'd circle the room two or three times, trying to find something to do. In the end he'd come to stand near the window, intending to look out at his pickup truck, but he'd see his own image reflected, and his eyes would dart away.

$\mathcal{H}$azel
Baker

She's my aunt by marriage, except Uncle Grady's dead. He died two years ago September. The Mr. Quik he owned was about to go under—7-Eleven had come to town—and Hazel says it worried him into the ground. But age had something to do with it. He was sixty-three, the same as Dad was when he died. Both of them had heart attacks, so it's reasonable to think I will one day too. I figure I've got about twenty-five or thirty years left.

Hazel's tall and big-boned and in her early fifties. She has auburn hair and dark brown eyes. She's got one daughter, who's just a couple of years younger than I am—she's married and living out West.

Hazel always wears Levi's, the kind that are bright blue and stiff as a board. When her jeans start looking just a little bit washed out, she gives them to the Goodwill store. She says it helps the cotton farmers out when she buys more.

She omits two or three syllables when she says "Indianola, Mississippi," the name of our hometown, and she pronounces "Alabama" as if it ended in *er*. What I'm saying is that Hazel spent just one semester at the junior college. But I've taught American History in high schools for thirteen years, and I believe she's a good bit smarter than most of the people I've worked with.

There's a little brown mole right beneath her left eye. Tonight, as she moves around the kitchen in my apartment, cooking a pair of chicken fried steaks and some mashed potatoes that I fully aim to inundate in gravy, I think about that mole and the day I joined the church.

I was eight then, which means that Hazel must have been

about twenty-five. After I went down front and told the preacher I wanted Jesus to come into my heart—a bald-faced lie, by the way, I just couldn't live with being the only kid in my Sunday school class who hadn't joined—I had to stand near the altar and let everybody in the church walk by and shake my hand.

Uncle Grady was next to last. "Good luck," was all he said. He shook my hand, squeezing my fingers so hard he almost crushed them. Uncle Grady was an enemy of delicacy. He was a big man with a loud voice and a red face that turned plum-colored whenever he got angry.

Then it was Hazel's turn. When I looked up at her that day, a tear was just dropping off that mole. She bent over to hug me, and I was suddenly in the midst of sweet smells and soft breasts. Her hair brushed my face, and my knees turned spongy. I swayed.

Suddenly I looked forward to the day when I could claim I'd backslid and rededicate my faith. If I was lucky, she might hug me again.

"Oh, Kenny," she whispered into my ear, "I'm so happy for you. One day when you're older, I'll tell you what all the good Lord's done for me."

What the good Lord had done for her, I understood, was somehow connected to what had happened a few years ago in Jackson. She and Uncle Grady had been living there, running a grocery store. We used to visit them every three or four months. Then one day my father said that he and Mother were going to see them without me. Aunt Hazel, he said, had been hurt. As he explained it, she'd been walking into the store one day when a crazy man jumped out of a pickup truck and shot her in the stomach. I asked why the guy had done that, but my father would only say, "Being stark-raving mad's motive enough for most crimes." He said the police had to hunt the man down.

Hazel no longer attends church. Either the good Lord quit doing whatever it was He used to do for her, or else she decided she could get by without it.

She spends a lot of her free time with me. She started phoning and coming over when I moved back to town last year. I've gotten used to having her around. It's a normal thing, she maintains. We share the same last name.

"Okay," she says now, wiping her hands on her apron, "I guess it's as ready as it'll be."

I live in a one-bedroom apartment at the rear of Earlene's Flowers. Despite the fact that I've got a couple of lamps and an overhead light, the living room always seems dark. I share one vent with the flower shop, so the place normally smells like gladiolas. But right now the odor of fried steak is overwhelming.

I sit down across the table from Hazel. She pops the top on a can of Budweiser and hands it to me. She doesn't drink, but it doesn't bother her if I do.

"Eat up," she says, piling potatoes onto her plate.

While we eat I tell her about my day. "I spent an hour talking to the principal," I tell her. "I've got this student in one of my classes whose name is Larry Singer, and I've been worried about him because another kid told me his mother's left town. I'm afraid he's living on the street."

"His daddy's not around?"

"Could be," I say. "I don't think he knows who his daddy is."

"What makes you think he's living on the street?"

"His clothes used to be clean, but they've been looking worse and worse. He never used to eat much in the cafeteria. Now he packs it away. But it looks to me like he's losing weight."

She says, "Well, why don't you bring him home tomorrow. I'll feed him till he busts at the navel."

Hazel knows full well that almost all of my students are black. Unlike Biloxi, where I worked until last year, this is still a place where black people and white people tend to meet only in public. The notion that you'd invite a black person home to eat supper is one most folks in this town would find strange. But Hazel isn't most folks.

"Okay," I say, "I'll bring him."

"I don't mind washing his clothes either," she says, "but it'll be up to you to get 'em off him."

After supper we sit down on the couch and watch CNN. Larry King is interviewing Jimmy Swaggart. Jimmy's been in trouble again, this time in California.

I say, "Swaggart turns my stomach."

Hazel says, "There's nobody without a weakness. At least he can sing."

Along about nine she begins to yawn. She raises her arms over her head to stretch. She's wearing a navy-blue velour pullover, and when she stretches like that, her breasts rise up in bold relief. I blush, but she doesn't notice.

She's still a fine-looking woman. I keep thinking I should tell her she ought to move to Memphis, to Little Rock, New Orleans, Atlanta. Someplace where there would be some available men. Every time I start to do that, though, I end up thinking, *Who am I to advise?* And too, I wonder who I'd spend my time with if she left town.

"Guess I'll head on home," she says. "I've got to open up the store in the morning." She's the assistant manager now at Wal-Mart.

I get up and walk her to the door. Outside, it's chilly, and the air smells like defoliant. Across the highway, the sign at Fred's Dollar Store is still lit up. The mist in the air makes the white letters fuzzy.

"Hey," I say, "thanks a bunch for the supper."

"I like having somebody to cook for," she says.

I stand nearby as she gets into her car. My arms dangle loosely at my sides.

Aaron Henry High School is a set of redbrick buildings on B. B. King Road, the best street in the worst part of town. The buildings are pretty run-down. The walls and ceilings need painting, the johns are reluctant to flush, and about half the bulbs for the overhead lights are missing. Last year, somebody started shooting windows out, and there was a period back in January when we had to wear coats in the classroom. The maintenance men couldn't replace the glass fast enough.

Back in the early seventies, when I was a kid, I lived in fear of ending up here. My parents had sent me to the all-white private school, but Dad was a small-time farmer, and coming up with the tuition each year was a burden. He held on somehow until I was safely away at Ole Miss, mortgaging my future to school loans.

It's kind of ironic that when I did wind up at Aaron Henry, I was so grateful to the principal for hiring me that I broke down in his office. He's a nice old guy with an Ed.D. from Tuskegee. While I wiped my face, he laid his hand on my knee.

"Son," he said gently, "we've all made mistakes."

The mistake I had made was to loop my arm around the shoulders of a girl who was a student in one of my classes at Biloxi High. At one time she'd been a solid B student, but her grades had begun to drop, and she often seemed distracted. I stopped her after class one day and asked her to drop by my room that afternoon.

As it turned out, she was dying to talk. She sat down beside me and told me about her mother and her father. Her dad, she said, had a bad drinking problem, and she believed her mother might be seeing another man. Both parents stayed gone a lot, and when they did come home, they spent all their time yelling at each other or at her. I remember that the whole time we were talking, she held onto a Coke can. Coca-Cola Classic, the can said. Her fingertips whitened, she squeezed it so hard.

"Mr. Baker," she said, dipping her head, "I know I need help, but I don't know what kind."

I had never found her very attractive. I didn't find her attractive in that moment, just as I wouldn't have found myself attractive if it had been me who looked into the room a few seconds later, rather than the assistant principal. If it had been me who glanced into the room, my eyes would have told me: here sit two lost souls. One is seventeen, skinny, poorly dressed, with bad skin. She's destined to live in a mobile home, with a man who buys Milwaukee's Best and occasionally succumbs to wild rage. The other is in his thirties. He has a beer belly, his hair is thinning fast, his front teeth invite comparison to those of certain quadrupeds. The last woman who kissed him was probably his mother. He's destined to live with himself, and his task will be at least as hard as the girl's. Both of these people, my eyes would have told me, are already dead in the water.

Many of the kids who stare back at me now, as I open my textbook and begin another American History class at Aaron Henry High, are dead in the water as well. They'll lose hands or fingers on the kill line at the Southern Prime Catfish plant, they'll lose hearts, lungs, and lives in some alley off Church Street to Smith & Wesson and the Indianola Police Department.

I glance at Larry Singer. He's wearing the same clothes he wore yesterday: a plaid shirt with a couple of buttons missing and a pair of jeans that look as if they were recently used to mop up an oil slick.

"Larry," I say, "you know who invented the stoplight?"

"Mr. Baker," he says, "I don't know, but I can guess."

I begin every class with a question of this type. "Go ahead," I say.

He grins. "Some swishy-tailed nigger."

"An African American," I tell him.

"He probably invented it," Larry says, "just so's he could run it in whatever car he'd done stole."

About half the class laughs. Larry's a cut-up, always good for a joke, but unlike a lot of smartasses, he never makes snide remarks once a teacher starts his lecture.

"Okay," I say, opening the loose-leaf binder that contains all my notes, "let's talk about the Freedmen's Bureau." The Freedmen's Bureau, I tell them, was created in 1865 by an act of the U.S. Congress. The bureau had a difficult job: it was responsible for preparing four million African Americans—newly liberated slaves—to assume the rights and duties of citizenship.

"If you look at the journals and record books of those who worked for the bureau," I say, "you get an idea of how hard a job they had. They were trying to help people who until very recently had been treated like property, and a lot of the time communication itself was a problem. As an example, there's a journal entry by one Joshua L. Clemmings, a bureau official who worked down in Jackson. Clemmings writes that an ex-slave presented himself at the bureau offices asking when he could expect to receive his bureau. His former mistress had given him a lot of old clothes, he informed Clemmings, and he needed someplace to keep them. He knew the word *bureau*, of course, in a completely different context, as a synonym for *chest of drawers*. In his journal, Clemmings notes that when he told the man the bureau was an organization established to provide opportunities for freed slaves—hence the name Freedmen's Bureau—the man got mad. 'I don't want no opportunity,' he's supposed to have said. 'I want that piece of furniture I was promised.'

"A lot of the time," I say, "when we try to help people, we discover that they're not ready or willing to receive the aid we want to give. But that shouldn't stop us from offering it. For decades, the prevailing view of the Freedmen's Bureau was that it achieved little or nothing. Now historians see things differently. The existence of the Freedmen's Bureau did provide opportunities that would not otherwise have existed. And while not everyone was willing or able to take advantage of those opportunities, a number of people did."

By the end of the session, about one-third of the students are asleep. The others are passing notes around, drawing football plays on their desks, or staring out the window at the world they'll have to return to at three o'clock.

"Tomorrow," I say, closing my notes, "we'll discuss the impeachment of Andrew Johnson."

I stop Larry Singer before he can make his exit. "Listen," I say, "I'd like you to come home with me for supper."

We're standing near the wall. He grabs the crank on the

pencil sharpener and spins it two or three times. "Can't do it, Mr. Baker," he says.

"Why not?"

"Momma got a caterer trucking in a shrimp surprise."

"Come on," I say. "My aunt's cooking up a big meal."

We go back and forth for three or four minutes, until he finally sees there's no graceful way out.

I meet him at the flagpole at six o'clock. I suggested picking him up at his house, but he claimed he had a date in the afternoon. That might well be the truth. Several of the girls seem to be in love with him.

"Hey, Mr. Baker," he says. He opens the door and climbs in.

We head north on B. B. King. The farther away from the school we drive, the nicer the houses look. Finally we cross the C & G, pass the compress and the gin, and we're in the white part of town.

"Don't get over here too often," Larry says.

"What happened to the shrimp truck?"

"Aw, Mr. Baker, you know I was just shooting you some shit."

"You don't say."

"Sure enough. Never was no shrimp truck. Wasn't nothing but Momma'd bought a couple of big porterhouse steaks and I made the shrimp truck up cause I was scared you wouldn't think steak was nothing special."

"I was talking to somebody the other day," I say carefully, concentrating on the road as if it enthralls me, "and they told me they thought maybe your mother had skipped town. I don't guess that's the truth, though, not if she's been out buying steaks."

Something fierce flashes in his eyes. Larry's just sixteen and, as far as I can tell, harmless. But four or five years from now, after he's tired of working fifty-hour weeks for minimum wage at Southern Prime, after one too many Delta planters stares right through him, he might be a mean man to meet behind Piggly Wiggly after dark. *Mr. Baker*, I imagine him saying, poking me in the gut with his knife, *I want your pocketbook, your Mastercard, your life.*

As it turns out, I've underestimated Larry. He will never want my life. "You know who I was talking to today?" he says. "Coach Washington. He come dragging his fat self out the gym between third and fourth period, caught me and a young lady squeezing by the bleachers. He waddles over and says, 'Larry, I'll teach your ass to fool around during school.' And you know what I told him? I said, 'Coach, I already *know* how to fool around—you looking at the evidence of that.' I said, 'You want to teach somebody how to fool around, you need to check out Mr. Baker. Look to me like that man could *stand* some lessons.'"

My ears always give me away. They're elongated, like Lyndon Johnson's were, and quick to turn red.

Evidently Larry notices. He tries to shift the subject, but that's hard to do when there's basically one thing on your mind. "Hey," he says, "you know what that girl I was sugaring up to told me? She said, 'You make the nicest noises of any Singer in town.'"

Hazel's car is already parked outside my place. When I open the door, Larry sniffs the air. In an instant, I know I was right. This kid hasn't eaten a real supper for several days.

Hazel, who I associate with stiff Levi's and pullover blouses, is wearing a shiny black dress that rustles as she moves toward us. She's wearing gold-plated earrings, a pair of high heels. Seeing her like this, decked out in all the finery a Wal-Mart salary can buy, makes me wonder. What other sides to Hazel Baker are there?

"Hi, Larry," she says. "Supper's ready. I'll just go and wash up."

The bathroom door closes behind her. Larry stares at it a minute or two, then turns to me. "Big and pretty," he says. "Big and pretty."

Pork chops and blackeyed peas, collard greens and mashed potatoes. Lemon meringue pie for dessert. Larry has seconds, has thirds. He says he never knew white women could cook. He thought they ate everything from cans.

By the time we've finished eating, Larry Singer is virtually defenseless. While I make coffee, he and Hazel stand at the sink. He's wearing a polka dot apron. He washes, she dries.

"Larry," she says, wiping off a plate, "what's your momma do for a living?"

"Used to work at Southern Prime."

"Used to?"

"Don't no more."

"Where does she work?"

"Ain't sure about that."

"Do you know where she is?"

"Not exactly."

"Do you have any idea?"

He gnaws at his lower lip for a while. Then his pensive look segues into a smile. "She's on Earth," he says. "That much I can swear."

"Where you staying at?"

"Roundabouts."

"Roundabouts?" I say. "Is that in Sunflower County?"

He ignores me. "We still got our place," he tells Hazel. "Rent's paid up through the end of the month."

"You got any brothers or sisters?" she says.

"Had a bunch. They all gone."

"Where to?"

"Chicago. Detroit."

"What do you aim to do," I say, "when the rent runs out?"

"Mr. Baker," Larry says, dark hands submerged in suds, "I thought a historian supposed to look backwards. Seem like you spend too much time looking forwards, worrying about what ain't happen yet."

I decide to let Hazel do the talking—she seems to be having more luck.

"What about aunts or uncles?" she says.

"Got an aunt," he admits.

"Where?"

"Used to stay over close to Winona."

Hazel says, "We need to get in touch with her."

Larry's lips set in an angry line. "She ain't got no use for me. She don't study nothing but dipping snuff. She get to dipping full-speed, she got two snuffy rivers dripping out her mouth."

"Honey," Hazel says, "you can't live on the street and go without food. We'll have to find you someplace to stay at least till your momma comes back."

He pulls his hands out of the sink. White suds roll off his copper-colored arms. He looks from her to me, then back at her again. "I wouldn't mind moving in with you and Mr. Baker," he says. "I'd wash the dishes every time you cooked."

It's late when I drive Larry home. In the car, on the way to his place, he says, "She your natural-born aunt or'd your uncle win her for the family?"

"My uncle Grady married her. He's dead now."

"If he's dead," Larry says, "aunt ain't what she is. She done quit being that and started being something else." He eyes me. "Question is, what?"

"Friend," I say.

"What kind of friend?"

"A good friend."

He lives in an apartment at the edge of town. It's in a dingy building that overlooks a cotton field. Somebody's picking cotton tonight, I can see the lights of a big four-row rig about a half mile away.

"Good night," I say.

Larry opens the door and gets out, then sticks his head back in. "Mr. Baker," he says, "I didn't aim to act like I didn't appreciate you asking me over to eat."

"I didn't take it that way."

"How come you worrying about me?"

I've asked myself that same question. There's an easy enough answer: that a teacher ought to worry about the welfare of his students. But I know that isn't the whole truth, and I know it won't satisfy Larry.

Once again I remember that girl in Biloxi, the way her voice sounded when she said *I know I need some help, but I don't know what kind.*

"I'm writing a book," I say.

Larry pulls his head back, like Muhammad Ali dodging a blow by Smokin' Joe. "Do what?"

"That's right," I say.

"What kind of book?"

"A history book."

"History of what?"

"Great lovers of the twentieth century. It'll have a whole chapter titled 'Larry Singer's Incredible Evenings.'"

"Aw, Mr. Baker," he says, "you shitting me."

"Good night," I say. "See you in the morning."

I intend to drive home. But if I've learned one thing in thirty-five years, it's this: what I intend to do and what I do are often not the same thing. I intended to be a college professor, but I'm teaching high school history. I intended to leave the Delta for good, but I'm living ten miles from the house where I grew up. I intended to have a family by now, but I'm still a bachelor, the sort of guy a sixteen-year-old kid might give a few useful tips to.

Is it any wonder, then, that I intend to drive home but don't? Before I know it, I'm cruising down West Gresham. I stop opposite a small dark bungalow. Hazel's old Chevy stands parked in the drive. It's past eleven. She's probably in bed.

When I was three or four years old, my parents took me to Jackson to attend the state fair. Afterwards, they wanted to go to a picture show, so they left me with Aunt Hazel and Uncle Grady. My cousin Mattie was just a baby then, and I remember rolling a miniature John Deere tractor across the floor while Aunt Hazel sat on the couch in the living room and nursed her. When she finished she handed Mattie to Uncle Grady, buttoned up her blouse and walked into the hall.

For whatever reason, I followed. I found her in the bathroom. Her blouse was unbuttoned again. She was standing near the sink, holding a long glass tube to her breast. Her lips were slightly parted, her eyes shut tight. With thumb and fore-finger she coaxed milk from a large pink nipple.

She must have heard me, because she opened her eyes and glanced at me. But my presence did not seem to bother her. She went right on with what she was doing. "This is a breast pump," she said. "And I'll tell you something, Kenny. It's a real life-saver."

Finally she pulled the tube away. A single drop of watery milk clung to her nipple. I watched, riveted, as it hung for a second, then fell toward the floor.

The next morning, before school, I pick up the phone to call Hazel. My heart is pounding so hard I can actually see the front of my shirt rise and fall.

She answers on the second ring. Her voice sounds murky—she was probably still in bed.

"Hi," I say. "You know what I was wondering? There's a football game tonight. Do you want to go?"

"I've got to work late tonight. One of my cashiers is taking off."

"How late?"

"Till seven-thirty."

"The ball game's at eight."

"Well," she says, "if you're not scared we'll miss the begin-ning."

After school I spend an hour taking a shower and getting dressed. When I finish, it's just six-fifteen. I decide to have a drink. I open a new bottle of Jack Daniel's and pour myself about half a glass. It's gone at 6:45. I return to the bathroom, open the medicine cabinet, and take out a bottle of Scope. I gargle for a couple of minutes. In high school, on those rare occasions when I embarked on a date, I would open my father's closet, pull out his half-pint of Old Crow, and slosh a little on both my cheeks. Back then, I wanted my date to think I was a hard-drinking man who just had to have a couple of shots to unwind. Now I want my date to think otherwise.

The difference is I'm thirty-five, not eighteen, and my date tonight is my aunt.

Or ex-aunt, as my mentor, Larry Singer, would see it.

She pulls into the yard at ten till eight. She rolls down the glass and says, "Your car or mine?"

"Yours," I say. "No, wait a minute. Mine."

We park on the shoulder of B. B. King, about a quarter of a mile from the school. I can hear the band playing the fight song. There's a November chill in the breeze. It carries with it the smell of hotdogs.

While we're walking toward the stadium, Hazel says, "We should've brought Larry. I doubt he's got money for a ticket."

The side of the road is rough, pockmarked. A couple of times Hazel stumbles, and her shoulder jostles mine. Once I grasp her elbow to steady her.

The fingers of her other hand close briefly over mine. An electrical current shoots up my spine. I pull my hand away.

"There's the kickoff," I say.

She says, "I don't know much about football."

My mouth begins to run as if it's nuclear-powered. I hear myself say that Aaron Henry High is at present 8-0, that we have an excellent chance to win the Delta Valley Championship, might even win the state title. I explain the theory behind the one-back offense, a subject about which I know nothing.

I buy our tickets, and we stand in front of the bleachers, looking for a place to sit. In the lights overhead, a thousand moths flutter. The band is blowing hot on "The Horse."

A girl from one of my classes waves and yells. "Hey, Mr. Baker, you can come sit with us."

I see her, about four rows up, sitting with several more girls. They're all wearing maroon letter jackets.

"We want to get a little bit higher," I holler.

"Don't you all get too high!" she shouts back. "Get too high, ain't no telling what you all liable to do."

The girls with her all burst out laughing. I grab Hazel's hand and pull her along the concrete walkway.

"There were places back there," she says.

"I'd rather not sit with my students."

There's one big empty space in the corner of the bleachers, fifteen or twenty rows up. We've got a lot of room to work with up here, and Hazel sits down about two feet away. But the wind is from the west, and it's not long before I get a whiff of her. She smells clean, smells fresh, smells of soap and springtime. Essence of Aunt, I christen her odor.

Down on the field, twenty-two young black men are doing their best to pound one another senseless. Shoulder pads pop, the linemen grunt and groan. *"Dig, dig, dig,"* yells a coach. A few rows away from us, an old man exhorts a player named Johnson to knock a snot bubble from his opponent's nose.

Surrounded by noise and action, by two thousand people who are stamping and shouting and otherwise making fools of themselves, I suddenly feel as if I could strip down to my underwear without attracting inordinate attention.

Emboldened, I say, "I guess this is a good sport for somebody that craves contact."

Hazel says, "I guess so."

In the silence that follows, I study her profile. She never wears much makeup. Just a little bit of rouge on her cheeks. Her skin is still smooth, her lashes are long.

"Maybe I ought to take it up," I say.

"Take what up?"

"Football."

"How come?"

"Because," I say, unable to shoo the tremor from my voice, "I crave contact."

She doesn't say a word. For a second I wish I were concrete. Then she slides over until we're sitting hip to hip, shoulder to shoulder, and before I have time to think about what's happening, her arm has encircled my waist.

It's only there for a minute or two, but we sit side by side for the rest of the game. The warmth of her body seeps through my windbreaker. From time to time, I believe I feel her heartbeat.

Afterwards, in the car going home, my hands are so damp I have trouble clutching the wheel. Hazel is silent. She hugs her armrest.

I pull into my yard and walk around the car to open her door. She gets out, then stands there staring at the ground. I can't think of anything to say. I recall Joshua L. Clemmings and the ex-slave who said, *"I don't want no opportunity."*

Then I focus on the brown mole. "I love that mole," I tell her.

She reaches up and touches it. "When I was younger," she says, "I intended to have it removed."

"Why didn't you?"

"Somebody asked me not to."

"Uncle Grady?" I say.

"No," she says. "Somebody else."

Because I can now think of nothing to talk about that doesn't involve the mole and because I refuse to ask who the somebody was, I say, "Whenever I see that mole, I think about the day I joined the church."

"The church?"

"You came down and hugged me," I say, "and you were crying a little bit, and when I looked up at you, a tear was just dropping off the mole."

Lines form near the corners of her mouth. "You remember that far back?"

"Sure."

She shakes her head. "God," she says, "you were just a child."

"I even remember what you told me."

"Then you've got a better memory than I have."

"I'm a historian," I say. "You said that someday you'd tell me what the good Lord had done for you. You never did tell me, though. You still haven't."

Once, when I was in college, I saw part of an old building collapse. The building had been a dormitory at one time, but it had stood empty for more than thirty years. A column caved in, and several tons of brick and mortar crashed down.

A similar thing happens to Hazel's face right now. "It's late," she says, backing away. "Good night, Kenny. Let's you and me talk history another time."

For a certain sort of person, Saturday mornings can be harsh. Look backwards and you're facing Friday night, when you sat in the living room rereading volume one of *The Americans*. Look forward and you're facing Saturday night, when you'll finish volume one and take up volume two. You can feel good about reading Daniel Boorstin on Sunday, Monday, Tuesday, Wednesday, or Thursday night, when almost everyone else you know is staked by an invisible chain to a glass-fronted cube that's been stuffed full of wires and tubes in Seoul or Tokyo. But on Friday and Saturday nights you do not belong in the house and you know it, and no matter what you've read or how originally you think you thought about it, on Saturday morning you have to confront the truth. Something's wrong, and you're the one it's wrong with.

But this Saturday morning will be different, because today I have something to accomplish. I get up, eat breakfast, slurp a cup of coffee down, and climb into my car.

The apartment building where Larry Singer lives looked a lot better after dark. There's graffiti on the dumpsters, and the sidewalks are buckled. Laundry flaps off the balcony railings. The cars, mostly Fords and Chevies, are old enough to be in graduate school.

I check the building directory, then climb the stairs to 2 E. Larry answers after I've knocked for two or three minutes.

"Mr. Baker," he says, rubbing sleep from his eyes.

I look past him into the apartment. Clothes are scattered there—dirty jeans, underwear, a T-shirt or two, some socks and tennis shoes. Otherwise, there's nothing except one old ratty-looking sofa. No TV, no stereo, no dining table.

He steps out, pulls the door closed behind him.

"Heard from your mother?" I say.

He stares off into the parking lot. He's too sleepy, I guess, to act cheeky. Or maybe he was hoping and now he's given up. "No sir," he says. "Doubt I will."

"So what are you up to today?"

"Wasn't up to nothing. I was in the bed."

"You want to take a little trip with me?"

"Trip to where?"

"Oxford," I tell him. "Ole Miss."

"I don't have no use for no Ole Miss," he says.

It's a quarter past eleven when we pull into Oxford. Larry is wide awake now, having drunk the sixteen-ounce coffee that I bought him at the Mr. Quik in Ruleville. In addition, he's just eaten the best breakfast he's had a chance at in two or three weeks, a six-pack of sugar-coated donuts.

I haven't been here in almost fifteen years. I left the day I graduated, and up until this moment, there's been no need to come back. I wonder if the trailer I used to live in is still around. It was out on Taylor Road, and I shared it with a born-again. On Saturday nights I lay in my bed at the end of the trailer, listening while he argued in the living room with his girl-friend. They fought about the Bible. She was a non-literalist. I used to envy them a lot.

I turn off Highway 6 and drive into the campus. It's de-serted, because the Rebs are playing LSU in Baton Rouge this evening. I park on the road that rings the Grove.

I pull ten dollars out of my wallet and hand the money to Larry. "Listen," I say, "I'm going to the library to do a little research. The student union's over there on the other side of the Grove. Why don't you walk around and take a look? There's no reason why you can't go to college if you want to. You can get student aid—I'll help you. If you don't like it here, you can go someplace else."

When I walk away, he's still sitting in the car, staring at the money in his hand.

The Ole Miss library has only changed a little. They've got electronic detectors now to catch you stealing books, and a notice posted out front says the building is open on Saturday night. Otherwise it's the same as it was fifteen years ago. A picture of Faulkner still hangs in the foyer.

I walk up to the circulation desk and ask the clerk where the microfilm is. He directs me to the basement.

I stroll along the banks of gray metal cabinets until I find the J's. They've got the Jackson paper in about thirty separate drawers, dating all the way back to the 1830s. I pull out the one containing reels for January of '61 through May of '64. There's no index, so I carry five boxes over to a viewer and attach the first spool to the feeder.

Most of the front-page articles concern the Civil Rights movement, and many of the headlines look like David Duke wrote them: "Four Negroes Enter Restaurant on State Street." . . . "Governor Barnett Confronts Noisy Colored Mob." Fingering the switch, I keep the film rolling, scanning the pages as they ascend the screen.

It's on the third reel, on the bottom half of a front page. The issue is from early November of 1962. On the top half of the page, there's a picture of James Meredith, the first black student at Ole Miss. In the photo, Meredith is walking out of the very building I sit in. He's accompanied by four U.S. Marshals, all packing sidearms.

On the bottom half of the page, there's a small snapshot of a man in his thirties, a man with thinning hair, a weak chin, the shadow of a beard on gaunt cheeks. The caption says *Lawrence Belton in June of last year.* Next to that photo, there's another. In this one, three medical orderlies are loading a stretcher into an ambulance while several city cops look on. One bare foot juts out from under the sheet. That's all you can see of Hazel Baker.

The headline says "Drifter with Troubled History Shoots Woman in West Jackson."

> Yesterday afternoon Hazel Baker, 21, of Jackson was shot outside the grocery store she and her husband own and run in West Jackson. The assailant, Lawrence Belton, a 32-year-old drifter who was occasionally employed as a garage mechanic, was later shot and killed by police as he fled the scene in a pickup truck. Mrs. Baker is in critical condition at Memorial Hospital.

A witness said that immediately prior to the shooting, the pickup truck, driven by Belton, had pulled into the parking lot behind the grocery store and Mrs. Baker had gotten out on the passenger side.

Dorothy Louise Ingram, a frequent customer at the grocery store run by the Bakers, said that when Mrs. Baker opened the door to get out of the truck, she heard Belton curse.

"He used a four-letter word," said Ingram, a resident of Raymond who comes to Jackson once a week to buy groceries. "Then he said, 'I'm not some old stray you can feed and close the door on.'"

Ingram said that Mrs. Baker stuck her head back in and said something that Ingram couldn't hear. At that point, Ingram leaned into the trunk of her own car, which was parked nearby.

"I was sticking a grocery sack under the turtle-shell," Ingram said, "so I never did see him pull the gun. But I heard it, I tell you. Sounded like a cannon going off."

Police said Belton fired two rounds from a .38-caliber revolver at Mrs. Baker, striking her once in the stomach. He then drove out of the lot at high speed.

Patrolman Stan Patterson noticed the pickup speeding on West Bates and pursued it. At the same time, he heard the radio report of the shooting and the description of Belton's vehicle.

Patterson and another officer, Patrolman Tommy Tegel, were following when Belton lost control of the pickup and smashed into a parked car as he attempted to turn onto Terry Road.

"He hopped out of the truck and took off," Patterson said, "and me and Tommy both advised him to halt. When he didn't, we didn't have no choice but to open fire."

Belton was pronounced dead on arrival at Memorial Hospital.

One of Belton's neighbors at a low-cost apartment house on Livingston Road said that Belton had told him he suffered from seizures and had been hospitalized for mental problems in Louisiana.

"I'd say he had a worried mind," said Wilburt Davis, who lived in the apartment next to Belton's. "I used to hear him out working on his truck in the parking lot in the middle of the night. He'd sing sometimes, mostly stuff by Hank Williams."

Neither Davis nor clerks questioned at Baker's Food Store could shed any light on Belton's motives. Mrs. Baker's husband, Grady, 34, was not available for comment.

But as I walk across campus toward the Grove, I wonder what, in the end, Uncle Grady could have said. Lost men were magnets, they tugged Hazel Baker's heart. Pity fell from her like rain. It had soaked him, and it had soaked Lawrence Belton. Now a few drops have fallen on me.

Larry Singer is leaning against the front of my car, the ten-dollar bill still clenched in his fist. "I don't like this place," he says. "They think it's Fort Sumter or what? Rebel flags everywhere."

"Larry," I say, "will you eat supper with me tonight? We can go over to my place then and watch a ball game or something. I'll buy us a six-pack."

A storm starts brewing in his eyes. "Mr. Baker," he says, "I think you ought to been a preacher. You wantin' to try to save me again?"

"No," I say, "I just want some company."

"That's all?" he says.

I say, "That's everything."

$\mathscr{C}$redits

The Literary Review	"A Life of Ease"
Michigan Quarterly Review	"Stay-Gone Days"
The New England Review	"Mississippi History" and "Hazel Baker"
Quarterly West	"Black Angus"
Shenandoah	"The Tower"
The Southern Review	"Hungarian Stew"
Witness	"Hoe Hands"

"House of Health" first appeared in *The Hudson Review*.

Steve Yar[...] [...]tion of
stories. H[...] [...] the *Southern Review*, the
Hudson Review, Shenandoah, the *New England Review,* and other
distinguished literary magazines. Born in Indianola, Mississippi, he now teaches creative writing at California State University in Fresno.